As soon as Hud stopped the vehicle, Audra hurried out from cover and into the passenger seat.

She leaned back, eyes closed. "I've never been so terrified in my life," she said.

"Yeah." He reached back and pulled two bottles of water from the cooler on the floorboard and handed one to her. "I need to report this and get some people out here to investigate. Do you want me to get someone to take you home?"

"No." She opened her eyes. "I'd rather stay here with you."

"I'd rather have you here." For a little while longer, at least, he needed to see her, to know for sure that she was all right.

"Why do you think he left?" she asked.

"I don't know. Maybe he never intended to kill us, only to scare us away. Maybe he got cold feet about killing a cop. Or a woman."

She hugged her arms across her stomach. "Scare us away from what? We haven't figured out anything."

"And someone wants it to stay that way."

MOUNTAIN INVESTIGATION

CINDI MYERS

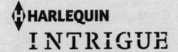

For Lucy.

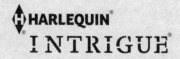

Recycling programs for this product may not exist in your area.

ISBN-13: 978-1-335-40158-8

Mountain Investigation

Copyright © 2021 by Cynthia Myers

This edition published by arrangement with Harlequin Books S.A.

For questions and comments about the quality of this book, please contact us at CustomerService@Harlequin.com.

Harlequin Enterprises ULC
22 Adelaide St. West, 40th Floor
Toronto, Ontario M5H 4E3, Canada
www.Harlequin.com

Printed in U.S.A.

Cindi Myers is the author of more than fifty novels. When she's not crafting new romance plots, she enjoys skiing, gardening, cooking, crafting and daydreaming. A lover of small-town life, she lives with her husband and two spoiled dogs in the Colorado mountains.

Books by Cindi Myers

Harlequin Intrigue

The Ranger Brigade: Rocky Mountain Manhunt

Investigation in Black Canyon
Mountain of Evidence
Mountain Investigation

Eagle Mountain Murder Mystery: Winter Storm Wedding

Ice Cold Killer
Snowbound Suspicion
Cold Conspiracy
Snowblind Justice

Eagle Mountain Murder Mystery

Saved by the Sheriff
Avalanche of Trouble
Deputy Defender
Danger on Dakota Ridge

The Ranger Brigade: Family Secrets

Murder in Black Canyon
Undercover Husband
Manhunt on Mystic Mesa
Soldier's Promise
Missing in Blue Mesa
Stranded with the Suspect

Visit the Author Profile page at Harlequin.com.

CAST OF CHARACTERS

Audra Trask—Dane Trask's daughter runs a day care center and keeps her head down. But when someone reveals secrets from her past in an attempt to smear her good name, she is determined to fight back.

Mark "Hud" Hudson—The Ranger Brigade tech specialist is part of the manhunt for Audra's father, Dane, but he's drawn to the strong young woman who refuses to let bullies win.

Dane Trask—This former army ranger has disappeared in the wilds of Black Canyon of Gunnison National Park. Why did he leave his job as a successful engineer for TDC Enterprises and abandon those who care about him?

Mitch Ruffino—The TDC vice president alternately praises and condemns Dane Trask and has offered a large reward for his capture. Is he behind the harassment of Audra?

Jana Keplar—The newest teacher at Canyon Critters Daycare doesn't hide her resentment of Audra and is sure she could do a better job of running the school. But how far would she go to get rid of her rival?

Chapter One

DEA officer Mark "Hud" Hudson liked his work. He liked having a job he believed in, one that stopped people from doing bad things and protected innocent people. A few times people he had arrested had even turned their lives around, and he liked to think he had had a hand in that.

But he didn't like dealing with people like the man in front of him right now. Dallas Wayne Braxton was a big, belligerent man whose bigness and belligerence had been only slightly diminished by the broken arm, two broken ribs, broken nose and two black eyes he had suffered. He stared out of his swollen face with the eyes of an angry animal, but spoke like a whiny child. "He just came out of nowhere and attacked me," he said, addressing Hud and fellow Ranger Brigade officer Jason Beck. "He's a dangerous lunatic. You people need to stop him."

"Him" was Dane Trask, an environmental engineer who had disappeared in Black Canyon of Gunnison National Park six weeks before, after sending his late-model pickup truck over the canyon rim. Since that time, Trask had been accused of embezzling large sums of money from his former employer, TDC Enterprises; stealing food and other items from campers in the park; and evading capture despite a large-scale manhunt involving officers from every law enforcement agency in the county.

"What were you doing in the park, Mr. Braxton?" Beck asked.

"I was hiking. This guy came out of nowhere and attacked me."

"You were hiking with a Ruger semiautomatic pistol in a shoulder holster under your jacket," Hud said. The park rangers who had responded to Braxton's call for help had relieved the injured man of the weapon.

"It's been all over the news how dangerous this Trask character is," Braxton said. "He's already murdered that girl hiker. I have a right to protect myself."

"Dane Trask did not kill the woman who was murdered in the park last month," Hud said. "That was another man." Though Trask may very well have killed, the Rangers had no proof he had committed murder. "And carrying a weapon in a national park is illegal."

"You're going to give me a hard time about that when this man almost killed me?" Braxton tried to sit up in his hospital bed, but fell back with a groan. "I'm not believing this. Whose side are you on?"

"Tell us again what happened," Beck said. "Just so we're sure we have all the details."

Braxton stuck out his lower lip, and Hud thought he was going to argue some more, but instead, he said, "I was hiking along, enjoying the nice day, and this guy jumped me. He came at me from the side of the trail, grabbed me around the neck and started whaling on me with a big stick. Kind of a club, you know? He broke my arm and my ribs. I swear, he was trying to kill me."

"But he didn't kill you," Hud said. "Why not, do you think?"

"Something must have scared him off," Braxton said.

"Did you draw your weapon?" Beck asked.

"I didn't have time. I tell you, he came out of no-where."

Hud consulted his notes. "The park ranger said he found your gun lying on the trail."

"It must have fallen out in the struggle." Braxton wouldn't meet Hud's gaze.

Hud nodded to Braxton's right arm, swathed in a cast. "Are you right-handed?"

"Yeah. So are a lot of people. What does that have to do with anything?"

"I was just thinking that if Trask wanted to kill you, the fastest way would have been to shoot you," Hud said. "We have reason to believe he's armed."

"He's crazy. Who knows why he does what he does?"

"Or maybe you saw him first," Beck said. "You drew your weapon and he struck your arm, break-ing it and preventing you from shooting him. Then he punched you and broke your nose. You broke the ribs when you fell back. Then Trask ran away."

"Are you calling me a liar?" Braxton's face flushed, a pulse pounding in his temple.

Hud met and held his gaze. "Did you go to the park today looking for Dane Trask?" he asked.

"What if I did? There's no law against that. And there's a $25,000 reward for his capture. Why shouldn't I get that money?"

Hud bit back a groan. That reward had caused nothing but trouble for law enforcement since TDC Enterprises had offered it. TDC had bombarded the media with announcements about the reward and plastered the town with posters, bringing every would-be bounty hunter to the park to stalk the trails and campgrounds, causing at least as much trouble as Trask ever had. TDC ostensibly wanted Trask found because he had embezzled $50,000 from them, but it seemed a lot of time and effort to expend when TDC made millions, or even billions, in profits every year.

"We don't have any other records of Trask attacking hikers, or campers, or anyone in the park or out of it," Hud said. "So I'm asking you again—what happened on that trail?"

Braxton looked away. "I had him dead to rights. I was on the trail and he stepped out in front of me."

"How do you know it was him?" Beck asked.

"I asked him! I drew my Ruger, told him to stop right there and I asked him. 'Are you Dane Trask?' He fit the description and the pictures on the posters, but I wanted to be sure. I'm not stupid."

Doubtful, Hud thought, but kept that opinion to himself. "What did he say?"

"He said 'Yes, and you need to go away and leave me alone.' Like that was going to happen. I told him he needed to come with me, then he took the big walking stick he had and went after me. It's lucky I'm still alive."

If Dane Trask, a former army ranger, had wanted to kill this man, he would be dead, Hud thought. "Is there anything else you'd like to tell us?" he asked.

"When you find him, you charge him with assault and attempted murder and grievous bodily harm. And I'm going to sue him for everything he's got."

"In the meantime, you'll be charged with carrying a concealed weapon without a permit and possession of a firearm within a national park."

Braxton's shouts of rage followed them down the hall and out of the hospital. Hud stopped beside the Ranger Brigade cruiser to inhale the non-antiseptic smells of hot asphalt and blooming lilacs. "If this keeps up, someone is going to end up dead," Beck said. "What does Trask think he's doing, running around in the park like Sasquatch or something?"

That was the question they'd been asking ever since park rangers had discovered Trask's late-model pickup at the bottom of the canyon, without Trask in it. A man with a good job, a good reputation, family and friends, had abandoned it all to hide in the wilderness, reappearing sporadically to send cryptic clues that seemed to implicate his former employer, TDC Enterprises, in some kind of shady goings on. But none of the clues were very clear, and the game had long since gotten old for everyone, it seemed, but Trask.

BAD THINGS COULD happen any day of the week, but when they happened on Mondays, somehow that made them worse. Audra Trask thought this when she saw the woman waiting outside her office that Monday morning, the first of June. A parent, though Audra couldn't put a name to the face this early in the day, and not a happy one, judging by the stiff posture and deep frown lines on the woman's otherwise attractive face.

It could be worse, Audra reminded herself, gathering herself for whatever confrontation was to come. Instead of a parent waiting for her, it could have been police, with more bad news about her father. Dane Trask had been missing—and wanted by the police— since mid-April. Every day Audra dreaded hearing he had either been found or was dead. Sometimes, she didn't know which would be worse.

"Good morning," Audra said as she moved past the woman to unlock her door. "What can I do for you?"

"It's what you need to be doing for my little girl," the woman said. She followed Audra into her office. "I enrolled her in this school because my friends raved about you. I had my doubts when I saw how young you were, but I decided to give you the benefit of the doubt, but now I see you clearly don't have any idea how to manage young children."

"Mrs. Patrick, please sit down and tell me what's wrong." Thank goodness, the woman's name had popped into Audra's head. "Has something happened with April?" April Patrick was in the four-year-old class with Jana Kepler as her teacher. Jana was new to the preschool, but she had come highly recommended.

"April is being bullied!" The word burst from Mrs. Patrick like a bullet from a rifle. She pressed her lips together, eyes shining with unshed tears. "I knew she'd been acting a little different these past two weeks, but I thought she was still recovering from the cold she had over Easter break. But when I picked her up Friday evening, she was crying. It took me two days to get her to tell me what was wrong."

"I promise you, we take bullying very seriously," Audra said, struggling to keep her voice calm. "I want you to tell me everything you know and I will get to the bottom of this."

Thus unfolded a story of another girl, Mia Ramsey, who had begun teasing April. At first it was simple mimicry, repeating everything April said in a whining tone. Then Mia began calling April names, and taunting when April cried. This progressed to pinching and hair-pulling—but only when no one else was around to see.

"Did April tell Mrs. Keplar about this?" Audra asked.

"She says she did, but Mrs. Keplar accused her of tattling and of being too sensitive."

Audra sat up straighter. If she had been a cartoon character, smoke would have come from her ears. "I will talk to Mrs. Keplar, and I will talk to Mia and her parents," she said. "I'm appalled that April had to endure something like this, and I'm also upset that this is the first I'm hearing of it. No child should ever have to experience something like that—especially under my care."

Mrs. Patrick's shoulders had relaxed, though she

continued to frown. "I hope so. I decided to keep April home today. She's with my neighbor, who used to sit for me before we enrolled in day care. I do think it's good for her to be around other children, but not if she's bullied."

"I promise I'll get to the bottom of this," Audra said.

She escorted Mrs. Patrick out of the office, but Audra's hands were still shaking when she sat behind her desk again. She pictured April, a pale, timid little girl who was smaller and quieter than most of her other classmates, exactly the sort who made an easy target for bullies. Audra had been a child like that, the girl who never fit in, who was teased and called names and made the butt of every joke. She had been older than April during the worst of it, but the scars had shaped her. She had had to fight for every bit of self-confidence she now possessed, but the conversation with Mrs. Patrick brought the old inner demons roaring back. Of course she wasn't capable of running this preschool, if she couldn't see a situation like this when it was right under her nose. Who did she think she was?

She took a deep breath and silenced those old tapes. She was capable of running this school, and she was exactly the person to handle this problem. She picked up her phone and called her assistant. "Brenda? Go to Mrs. Keplar's class and tell her I need to speak to her immediately. You can watch her class while she's with me."

"Sure," Brenda said, drawing out the word in a way

that conveyed her curiosity over this unusual summons, but Audra didn't offer any details.

A few minutes later, Jana Keplar stood in Audra's open doorway. A tall, strong-featured woman in her early forties with short dark hair streaked with gray, Jana had started working for the school in January, replacing a teacher who had decided to remain home with her newborn twins. Audra had been impressed with Jana's experience and with her enthusiastic teaching style, which students—and parents—seemed to love.

"This couldn't have waited until lunch?" Jana asked before Audra could speak. "It's very disruptive to my class to ask me to leave in the middle of a lesson."

"I didn't feel this could wait. Please, shut the door behind you and have a seat."

Jana shut the door, but she remained standing, "What's the problem?" she demanded.

"April Patrick's mother came to see me this morning," Audra said. "She told me April is being bullied. Naturally, she was very upset."

"April is entirely too sensitive," Jana said. "If she didn't cry every time anyone looked at her sideways, the other children wouldn't pick on her so. I've told her she should stand up to them, or at least ignore them, but she doesn't listen."

"Sit down." Audra was firm. "Please."

Jana hesitated, then sat, perched on the edge of the chair, back stiff, hands on her knees as if she was prepared to leap up again at any second.

"Mrs. Patrick said Mia Ramsey in particular targets April," Audra said.

"Mia is a very bright, outgoing girl who is very popular with the other children," Jana said. "I think April is jealous of her. She exaggerates the things Mia says and takes offense where none is intended."

"Mrs. Patrick says April told her Mia pinches her and pulls her hair. You know that is strictly against the rules."

Jana did not roll her eyes, but Audra had the sense she wanted to. "I've examined April and questioned Mia several times," she said. "But she swears she never touched April, and I couldn't find a mark on the child. If Mia really pinched her, it would leave a mark, don't you think?"

"It's important to take accusations like these seriously," Audra said. "We have a zero-tolerance policy when it comes to bullying."

"And it's just as important not to brand an innocent, perfectly pleasant child as a bully simply because some sniveling ninny is trying to get attention." Jana's voice rose and her knuckles blanched white as she gripped her knees.

"I won't allow you to label any child that way." Audra spoke sharply. "If I hear it again—and especially if I hear it in front of the children—you will be dismissed."

Jana paled and bowed her head. "I'm sorry. I'm frustrated with this whole situation and I let my frustration get the better of me. It won't happen again."

"I hope not," Audra said. "Perhaps it would be helpful if I talked to the girls."

Jana leaped up. "You don't need to do that. I was teaching children when you were still in diapers," she said. "I think I know how to handle a group of four-year-olds."

"Then handle it," Audra said, outwardly calm, but inwardly seething. She had long suspected that Jana, who had operated her own day care center in Kentucky, where she had lived before her husband transferred to Colorado, resented working as a teacher under someone so much younger. "Instead of telling April to ignore Mia, tell Mia to ignore April. Separate the children as much as possible. And keep an eye on them. I don't want any more complaints."

Jana glared at her. "Is that all?"

"Yes, that's all."

She left, closing the door very firmly behind her. Audra sighed. She didn't have a sense that anything she had said had changed Jana's mind, but then again, she didn't know the woman very well. The school she had run in Kentucky had gotten rave reviews. One of the parents Audra had contacted when checking Jana's references had even cried as she talked about how much her little boy missed his former teacher. That kind of experience had to count for something.

A knock on the door interrupted her musings. "Come in," she called.

Brenda stuck her head around the door. "Everything okay?" she asked.

"Everything's fine. How was the class?"

"Oh, they're a great bunch of kids," Brenda said. "They were learning a new counting song and the cutest little girl—Mia Ramsey—volunteered to teach it to me. Such a sweetie."

Audra's stomach clenched. A "sweetie" who might very well be a bully. But what if Jana was right, and April *was* making things up, or at least exaggerating, in order to get attention? Shy, awkward children, so used to being overlooked, did sometimes act out as a way to be noticed. Audra had done it herself.

Brenda had come all the way into the room now, and was watching Audra, looking apprehensive. "Is there something else?" Audra asked. Another Monday problem to tackle?

"Did you watch the news this morning?" Brenda asked.

Another knot in Audra's stomach. Since her father's disappearance, she avoided the news. "No. Why?"

Brenda winced. "There was a story about a man attacked in Black Canyon of Gunnison National Park. I guess he was hurt pretty bad. He says your father attacked him."

Audra held herself very still, keeping in all the emotions that battered against her insides. Her father, the man she had loved and depended on all her life, was now some wild man, lurking in the wilderness and doing crazy things. She didn't understand any of it. She hated all of it.

"I'm sorry," Brenda said. "I hated to tell you, but then I thought if one of the other teachers or a parent, or even a child, said something, you ought to be prepared."

"Thank you."

She expected Brenda to go then, but she didn't. "There's another reason I felt I should tell you," she said.

"Yes?" Could this really get worse?

"There's an officer out front who wants to see you. He didn't say, but I'm pretty sure it's about your father."

Audra closed her eyes. Of course the police wanted to talk to her about her father. It was that kind of Monday.

Chapter Two

Audra remembered Officer Mark Hudson as having a smile that would melt chocolate and a laugh that had set up a butterfly flutter in her chest. Add in thick blond hair and sky-blue eyes, and the sum was a man who, under other circumstances, Audra wouldn't have minded seeing again. But the handsome cop wasn't smiling now, and unlike the other times when he had questioned her about her father, today he seemed more forbidding than friendly. He entered her office and stood beside her desk, frowning down at her, the way a teacher might confront a student who had misbehaved.

She shook off the notion, straightened her back and spoke first. "I heard there was a news report that my father attacked someone in the park. Is that true?"

The frown lines on Hudson's forehead deepened. "A man was attacked early this morning. He says the person who attacked him was your father."

She curled her hands into fists, her fingernails digging into her palms. "That doesn't sound like Dad at all," she said softly.

Hudson pulled the visitor's chair closer to her, alongside the desk instead of across from it, and sat, the various items attached to the belt at his waist softly clanking and creaking as he did so. She caught the scent of his aftershave—something clean and woodsy—and felt disoriented. This man was hunting her father. He wasn't her friend, so she shouldn't be thinking about how good he smelled and looked.

She forced herself to look into his eyes. "Why are you here?" she asked.

"We need to find your father before more people are hurt," he said. "Or before someone hurts him."

She gasped. "What do you mean?" She had visions of officers going after her father with orders to shoot to kill. "I don't care what you say, I can't believe my father would deliberately hurt anyone. He's not like that."

"I'm sure he isn't like that with you," Hudson said. "But remaining on the run in the wilderness is the act of a desperate man. One who might do anything to avoid being caught."

"Then tell me why he'd attack a stranger," she said. "What does he possibly have to gain by that? Are you even sure it was him? After all, people thought he killed that hiker, Marsha Grandberry, and it turned out to be someone who was trying to frame him for the crime."

The murderer, Toby Masterson, had kidnapped her father's former girlfriend, Eve Shea, and tried to use her to lure Dane from hiding. After Masterson died, some people whispered Dane had killed him in order to save Eve, but that wasn't the same as the kind of unprovoked attack Officer Hudson was talking about.

"The man who was attacked says he asked the man he encountered if he was Dane Trask and the man said he was," Hudson said.

"So they had this conversation and then Dad just attacked him?"

"The man had a gun. I think he was injured when your father disarmed him. Your father did hurt him, but I believe he acted in self-defense. He probably could have killed the man if he had wanted to, but he didn't."

The relief that surged through her made her eyes sting with tears. "Why are you doing this?" she asked. "Why are you hunting him, like…like some wild animal? Why can't you just leave him alone?"

"Until we have him in custody, he won't be safe," Hudson said. "The reward TDC is offering for his capture has raised a lot of interest. People are coming into the park just to look for your father. The man he fought with today isn't the first one of those people to be armed. It's against the law to carry a weapon in a national park, but that hasn't stopped everyone."

"Then make TDC end the reward offer," she said.

"We don't have the authority to do that. They aren't breaking any laws. They may even think they're helping."

"I still don't see why you're here." She sat back, trying to put more distance between them. "You're wasting my time and yours."

"Are you sure your father hasn't been in touch with you?"

"No. I'd tell you if he had. Why are you even asking?"

"I'm asking because he contacted his former administrative assistant, Cara Mead, and his former girlfriend, Eve Shea. You're his daughter. It would be very natural for him to turn to you for help."

"I don't know why he hasn't contacted me, but he hasn't." Part of her was hurt that her father had turned to others for help instead of her. But she was also relieved. Whatever he was involved in, how could she possibly help him? She wasn't a lawyer or a cop. She ran a preschool for a living. "Look, Officer Hudson. I understand why you think I must have heard from my father, but I'm telling the truth."

"Call me Hud," he said. "Everyone does."

She looked away, unsure how to respond. He was being friendly, but how could he be her friend? "Maybe he hasn't contacted me because he's always been the one to help me," she said.

"How did he help you?"

She shrugged. "Just, you know—Dad things. He gave me advice. He lent me money when I needed it." *He drove me to rehab and paid for lots of therapy.* But that was personal, not anything the cops needed to know.

"He and your mother never married, is that right?"

He knew this. They had been over everything the first time he talked to her, right after her dad disappeared. But the cops always asked the same questions over and over, as if double-checking her answers. "My mother was Dad's college girlfriend," she said. "He offered to marry her, but she said no." She had asked her mother once why she'd said no. "We were young and stupid and we certainly weren't in love," her mother had replied. But she had gone on to marry two other men, and had, at least eventually, not been in love with them, either.

"Was he around much when you were growing up?" Hudson asked.

"All the time. He and my mom shared custody. For a while in high school I even lived with him full-time." Her mom had been married at the time to a man who didn't like Audra. The feeling had been mutual. "He was always there for me," she added.

"And it hurts that he's not here now."

She stared at him, stunned at his perception. "Yes." She swallowed. "Yes, it does. Which is why I'd do anything to help you find him if I could."

He nodded, though whether to confirm that he believed her or because she had given an answer he liked, she couldn't tell. "I've been thinking a lot about how he's managed to pull this off," Hud said. "I think he must have planned this ahead of time. He may have cached food and water in the park, and other supplies. Maybe he scouted out caves and other places he could use for shelter. Others have told us he spent a lot of time hiking in the park."

"It was one of his favorite places," she agreed.

"When did he go there?" Hudson asked. "How often?"

"He went on weekends or after work, but I don't think it was that often. Maybe once a month. It could have been more. I mean, we each had our own place, and we didn't see each other every day."

"Tell me again about the last time you saw him."

"I told you all this before," she said. "Don't you have it written down somewhere?"

"I do, but it's helpful to go over it again. You might remember something you didn't mention before, or something might stand out for me that I didn't pay attention to before."

"All right." She stared at the desk, trying to bring that day over seven weeks ago back into focus. "We had dinner the night before I left for vacation in Paris," she said.

"You went there to see friends, right?"

"Right. I'd been planning the trip for a couple of years, so I was really excited to go. I think that's why I don't really remember a lot about that night. Dad seemed normal to me, but if he wasn't, I might not have noticed. I wasn't really focused on him."

"What did you talk about at dinner?"

"We talked about Paris. He went there once, when he was in the military. He was stationed in Germany and went there on leave. He told me about the museums he visited and talked about places I planned to go. We talked about the friends I visited—Denise and Richie. Dad had met them a couple of times." She paused, then added, "We talked a little about the new school TDC is building near their headquarters. I won the contract for the on-site day care and preschool, and I was really excited about that."

"Did you father work on that project?" Hudson asked.

"I think he did the initial environmental assessment. Or someone in his department did, anyway. That happens way before construction, though, so he didn't have anything to do with the project once they broke ground."

"You mentioned before that he told you to be careful before he left you that night."

"Well, yeah. But I didn't think there was anything odd about it. He was always telling me to be careful. Parents do that. But then he said it again, and it did strike me as odd that he would say it twice, and so intently. I even joked about it, and asked him if he had some kind of presentiment that something terrible was going to happen."

"What did he say, exactly?"

"He said, 'I mean it, you be careful—in Paris, and after you get home.'"

"Anything else?"

"No." His expression of disappointment made her feel awkward, as if she'd failed him somehow.

"Did your father have a favorite place in the park?" he asked. "A place he liked to camp or hike?"

"No. That wasn't something we shared."

"You don't like to hike or camp?"

"I enjoy it, but I'm not into it the way Dad is. I thought it was fun for a night or two, but Dad would camp for a week or more." She stopped to fight back another wave of emotion. "I wonder if he thinks it's so much fun now."

"Maybe he enjoys the challenge. He trained for this kind of thing in the army."

"Maybe." She glanced at the clock, astonished to see it was after ten. "I really need to get to work," she said.

He stood and moved the chair back in front of the desk. "Thank you for your help," he said. "If you think of anything else, call me. Do you still have my card?"

"Yes." She had it tucked inside her billfold. Not that she intended to ever use it, but she liked knowing it was there. She stood also. "I have to get to playground duty," she said.

"You run this place and you have to do playground duty?" he asked.

"It's important for the students to get to know me, and it's a good opportunity to observe their interactions with one another and with the teachers. You can't really run a business if you sit behind a desk all day."

"Did your father teach you that?"

She smiled. "Yes, he did."

"We're not hunting him," he said. "Not like an animal, or like a criminal. When we find him, we want to help him. Only a desperate man would do what he's done."

"Why is he so desperate?" she asked.

"That's what we have to find out."

Hud should have been reviewing the case on the drive back to Ranger Brigade headquarters, but instead he found himself focused on Audra Trask. Barely five feet tall and fine-boned, she struck him as the sort of person others might underestimate on first meeting. Then again, maybe the real clue to her spirit lay in the abundant dark hair that swirled like a storm cloud about her head, the thick curls refusing to be tamed.

Of all the people associated with this case, she was the one he felt for the most. Of all the people Dane Trask had hurt with his disappearing act, Audra struck him as the most bereft, more confused than devastated just now, but if Trask continued these dangerous games, Audra might be the one who was most damaged by his actions.

He turned off the highway onto the road leading into Black Canyon of Gunnison National Park. The high desert of this part of southwest Colorado struck most first-time visitors as flat and uninteresting, without the majesty of the distant snow-capped peaks or the lushness of river valleys only a short drive away. The canyon that gave the park its name revealed itself with stark suddenness to those who parked at one of the many scenic overlooks along the roadway and took a short walk to the canyon rim. The chasm that opened at their feet split the earth like a knife gash cut into a lavish confection, layers of crimson and shell pink and silver plunging over three thousand feet to the slender silver ribbon of Gunnison River.

It was this wilderness—approximately 130,000 acres, including the park and two adjacent national recreation areas—that Dane Trask had chosen as his hideout. This was also the territory of the Ranger

Brigade, a unique, multiagency task force designed to fight crime on these vast public lands.

Hud didn't know if Trask had committed any crimes, but the man had disappeared in the Rangers' jurisdiction, so they were the ones tasked with finding him. The longer this one man eluded them, the more frustrating the case became.

He turned into Ranger headquarters, a low-slung building just inside the park entrance, and parked out front. He had scarcely exited his car when a man hailed him from across the parking lot. "Officer Hudson!"

An athletic man with windblown sandy hair trailing past his shoulders jogged over to Hud. "Roy Holliday," he said, offering his hand.

Hud didn't accept the handshake. He didn't know this man, and letting a stranger get you in his grip could be a recipe for trouble with the wrong person. "What can I do for you, Mr. Holliday?" he asked.

"I'm working on a story on the Dane Trask case. I wanted to ask you a few questions."

"I can't help you." Hud turned away, but Holliday kept pace with him as he strode toward headquarters.

"What about the attack on Dallas Wayne Braxton this morning?" Holliday said. "Braxton says Trask attacked him without provocation, but I heard his gun was found on the trail and his right arm was broken. That suggests to me that Braxton drew the gun and Trask broke the arm to keep him from firing. What do you think about that?"

He thought someone had probably spoken to the

reporter who shouldn't have. One of the park rangers, maybe? "No comment," he said.

"What about Audra Trask?" Holliday asked.

Hud stopped. "What about her?"

"She's Dane Trask's closest relative. She must know something she's not telling. Do you think she's covering for her father? Have you questioned her?"

"Ms. Trask doesn't know anything," Hud said. "You need to leave her alone."

"It's my job to talk to people," Holliday said.

"There's a fine line between talking and harassing," Hud said. "If you cross it, you'll have me to answer to."

"That's a mighty strong answer," Holliday said. "Do you and Ms. Trask have some kind of personal relationship?"

Hud cursed his inability to keep his mouth shut. "I'd say the same about any witness in this case," he said.

"So you admit that Audra Trask is a witness." Holliday pulled out a notebook. "Can I quote you on that?"

They had reached the door of the office. Rather than dig the hole he was in any deeper, Hud yanked open the door, ducked inside and shut it in Holliday's face.

"Your turn to run the gauntlet, I see." Officer Carmen Redhorse gave Hud a sympathetic smile. A slender woman of Ute descent, Redhorse had been with the Ranger Brigade since its inception two years ago and had grown up in the area. She'd been generous in sharing her knowledge with newcomers like Hud.

"Don't we have someone who's supposed to deal with the press?" Hud asked.

"I already gave him an official statement." Sheriff's deputy Faith Martin, the Ranger Brigade's official media liaison, looked up from her desk across the room. "I can ask him to leave, but you know I can't keep him off public property."

"I don't remember seeing him around before," Hud said. "Who's he with?"

"He's a freelancer," Martin said. "He's the one who broke the story this morning about the attack on Dallas Wayne Braxton."

"Beck told us you think Braxton went after Trask and Trask fought back," Redhorse said.

Hud nodded. "I'm sure part of Trask's army training was in disarming the enemy. Braxton is a blowhard who thought he had the upper hand because he had a Ruger in his hand. Trask probably broke his arm with one blow, then socked him in the face to send a message. Then he got out of there. If he'd wanted to kill the man, he could have. But he didn't."

"What did his daughter have to say?" Redhorse asked.

Hud shook his head. "She's worried about her father, but she doesn't know anything."

"Not anything she'll tell us, anyway," Redhorse said.

"I really think she doesn't know. Which doesn't do any of us any good."

"Trask seems to have it in for his former employer," Martin said. "All these cryptic clues he's left us—the environmental reports from the Mary Lee mine and the press release he tried to get his former girlfriend to give to the press—have to do with that mine. But how are a bunch of reports that may or may not be right be worth throwing away your whole life for?"

"You could say that TDC has it in for Trask, too," Redhorse said. "They've accused him of embezzlement and are offering that big reward for his capture."

"Whatever is going on, I wish they could have settled it with mediation or something sensible," Hud said. "How much time and money are we wasting, chasing after this guy?"

"There has to be more going on," Redhorse said. "Everything about Dane Trask's past says he's a smart, sensible guy."

"He's not acting smart or sensible now," Martin said.

Was Trask behaving so out of character on purpose? Hud wondered. If his own daughter had no explanation for his actions, how did the cops have a hope of figuring him out?

Chapter Three

Tuesday, Audra made a point of greeting April Patrick and her mother at drop-off that morning. "Hello, April." She squatted and looked the little girl in the eyes. "We missed you yesterday. I'm glad you're back."

April flushed and stared at her shoes. Audra turned to Mrs. Patrick. "I've spoken with April's teacher, and we'll be keeping a close eye on the situation."

"Thank you." Mrs. Patrick addressed her daughter. "Remember what we talked about," she said. "You're my wonderful girl."

Audra turned away, blinking back tears. Her father used to say that to her when he dropped her off at school in the mornings.

"Hello, Mrs. Patrick. April." Jana stepped between Audra and the girl. "How about I walk you to class?" She took April's hand and left, but Jana glanced back once, as if to say "See, I've got this."

April remained on Audra's mind the rest of the morning. At noon she walked down to the lunchroom, arriving just as Jana's class of four-year-olds filed in. April was easy to spot, lagging behind the others, head down. She sat at the end of the table farthest from Jana, an empty seat on either side of her. Audra's heart twisted at the sight of the child. She took the seat next to her. "Hello, everyone," she said.

"Hello, Ms. Trask," the children chorused. Jana merely frowned from the other end of the table.

"Hello, April," Audra said to the child next to her.

"Hello." April spoke so softly, Audra had to lean forward to hear.

"I thought you might like to come and eat lunch with me today," Audra said.

April stared at her, eyes wide. "Am I in trouble?"

"No, of course not." Audra looked at the other students. Everyone at this table, and those nearby, was watching. "I'm starting something new," Audra said, loud enough for everyone to hear. "I'm going to have lunch with a different student every week, in order to get to know you all better. We'll have a special table, over there." She pointed to a table in the far corner of the room. The only thing special about it was there was no one else seated at it. She stood and began gathering April's lunch things. "Come on, April, we'll have fun."

The little girl followed, head down, clearly less than delighted. Audra signaled to Mrs. Garibaldi, the lunchroom manager, and after a brief, whispered discussion, Mrs. Garibaldi hurried away, and Audra led April to the table. A few moments later, Mrs. Garibaldi returned with a tray that held two glasses of fizzy water with slices of oranges and lemons, a rose in a bud vase, and two little containers of vanilla ice cream. Ordinarily, the students had ice cream for dessert on Fridays, so Audra hoped this was enough of a special treat to ease April's fears that she was in trouble.

Audra unpacked her own sandwich and fruit. "Let's talk while we eat, okay?" she suggested.

April nodded and picked up her sandwich—peanut butter and strawberry jelly. A classic. "You remind me of me when I was a little girl," Audra said.

April stared and nibbled at the edge of her sandwich.

"I was very quiet," Audra said. "There's nothing wrong with being quiet, but sometimes the other children didn't understand. Sometimes they picked on me."

April put down the sandwich but remained silent. "Do other children ever pick on you?" Audra asked.

A shrug.

"When someone picks on you, they're being a bully," Audra said. "Have you heard that word before?"

April nodded.

"Bullying is wrong," Audra said. "I don't want any bullying in my school, so if anyone bullies you, I want you to promise to tell me. You can ask to be excused and come to my office anytime." That might be asking too much of the little girl, but Audra hoped just knowing she was ready to listen if April found the courage to talk to her might help.

"Okay," April said. She picked up her sandwich

and studied it. "Sometimes the other girls call me a baby."

"You're the same age they are, so you obviously aren't a baby," Audra said.

"They mean I act like a baby, because I cry a lot."

"It's hard not to cry when you're upset about something," Audra said. She resisted the urge to tell the girl to try harder not to cry. Adults had told Audra that over and over when she was a child, and it only made things worse. "Crying just makes you human, it doesn't made you a baby."

April looked as if she didn't quite believe this. "None of them cry as much as I do."

"Some people talk more than other people," Audra said. "Some people have a harder time sitting still in class. Some people are really good at running, while others can sing or tell stories or read better than everyone else. Some people like peanut butter and other people like tuna fish. Everyone is different. The world would be really boring if we were all alike."

"I guess."

Audra stifled a sigh. She didn't really blame the girl for not being persuaded. When you were a child, the adults around you had plenty of advice, but the only thing that really helped was to teach everyone to be kinder and more understanding. Audra could work on that. There were probably lots of anti-bullying programs out there. She'd find one and implement it at her school.

She checked her watch. Lunch was almost over. "Eat your ice cream before it melts," she told April.

"But I haven't finished my lunch," the girl said.

"That's okay. Today, if you want, you can eat the ice cream first."

To her delight, April smiled, a toothy grin that transformed her from pale and sullen to pink-cheeked and happy. Maybe, sometimes, ice cream worked better than talking.

AUDRA WASN'T SURPRISED when Jana came to her office after classes that day. "If you're going to take a child out of my class, you need to talk to me about it first," she said without preamble after Audra greeted her.

"I didn't take her out of class. I took her to another table at lunch."

"So you could get her away from me and talk." Jana dropped into the visitor's chair. "I asked her what you talked about, and she said you talked about bullying. Didn't you believe what I told you before?"

"This isn't about you," Audra said, trying to keep the frustration out of her voice. "I wanted April to know that if she has any problems, I'm another adult she can talk to."

"I'm her teacher. If she has a problem, she should come to me."

"Of course. But she needs to know there are other sympathetic adults in her life. I thought I would have lunch with Mia another day and hear her side of things."

"There's nothing wrong with Mia," Jana said. "She's just a strong-minded child who doesn't suffer fools gladly."

"Are you calling April a fool?"

"I didn't mean that and you know it," Jana said. "But people are too quick to label someone a bully. There's too much political correctness. Instead of babying children and catering to every whim, we ought to teach them how to deal with adversity."

"April and Mia are four years old!"

"They're privileged and spoiled. A few challenges in life would only do them good."

"That is for their parents to decide, not us."

Jana looked away. When she faced forward again, her expression was more composed. "Speaking of challenges, why was that cop here yesterday?"

"That doesn't really concern you," Audra said.

"It doesn't look good for the school to have cops hanging around. You ought to know that."

"I'll take care of the school. You take care of your class." Audra met the older woman's cold gaze with an icy stare of her own. Jana was older and more experienced and thought she knew better, but Audra sensed if she yielded to her, Jana would end up taking over. In that way, she was just another kind of bully. "You can go now," she added.

Jana went, and Audra waited a moment, collecting herself before she followed the older woman out the door. *You'd have been proud of me just now, Dad*, she thought as she walked to her car. *Please come home so I can be proud of you.*

ONE OF THE things that had struck Hud the most when he first became a law enforcement officer was how many people weren't glad to see him when he walked in the door. Most of them never said anything, but he had learned to recognize the averted eyes and shrinking back that signaled they'd be happier if he left. He had naively imagined that people would be grateful to him for keeping them safe and riding to their rescue. His first few weeks as a rookie had taught him otherwise.

But it stung a little more when the person averting her eyes or shrinking away was a woman he was attracted to. A woman like Audra Trask.

He was returning from transporting a prisoner to the county jail that evening when he spotted Audra's car ahead of his. When she signaled a turn onto a side street, he followed, and parked behind her when she pulled to the curb in front of a neat, stucco-sided duplex. She waited beside her car as he approached her. "Is there a reason you were following me?" she asked.

At five feet ten inches, he wasn't a tall man, but he felt oversize and clumsy next to her. She was so petite, but there was nothing childlike in the hard look she gave him. "I saw your car and I wanted to make sure you were all right," he said.

"Why wouldn't I be all right?" she asked.

"Other women who were close to your father have been threatened." Cara Mead had been. So had Eve Shea.

"No one's threatened me," she said. "Why would they?"

"One of the many, many unanswered questions in this case," he said.

She folded her arms in front of her. "You don't need to follow me," she said. "I'm fine."

"I wasn't following you." He took a step closer. "I just saw you and thought it might be nice to have a conversation that wasn't about your father."

"That's a line I haven't heard before. It's original, I'll give you that."

"It wasn't a line," he said.

"Wasn't it?" Her eyes held a challenge. He shifted his gaze from her dark brown eyes to her lips—full and tinted a dark pink. He felt a rush of heat that had nothing to do with the weather and thought of stepping back. Instead, he moved closer.

She didn't back up. Instead, she uncrossed her arms. In her right hand, she held her house keys. "You might as well come in."

He waited while she unlocked the door, then followed her into the western half of the duplex. The rooms were small and simply furnished, with white-painted walls and lots of green plants. The place was neater than it had been the first time he'd interviewed her, but then she had just returned from two weeks in France. She dropped her purse and briefcase on a table at the end of a red-upholstered sofa. "Would you like a glass of water?" she asked. "Or I could make tea."

"Water is fine." The kitchen was also small, but glass-fronted cabinets and a large window over the sink made it appear larger. She took a pitcher of water from the stainless refrigerator and filled two glasses, then handed him one. He waited for her to speak, but she didn't. He let the silence stretch until it was uncomfortable. "How was your day?" he asked.

"It could have been better," she said. "I'm dealing with a child who's being bullied, and that's upsetting."

"Is that a big problem in preschool?" He would have thought bullying was something older children faced, not toddlers.

"Sometimes. This child is the sort of shy, awkward girl that some kids target."

"A lot of bullies are hurting and lash out," he said.

"I see you've read the literature," she said. "Was that part of your law enforcement training?"

"Not exactly. What are you going to do about it?"

"I'm going to talk to both of the girls and try to help them. They're very young, so stopping this kind of behavior now can save a lot of trouble in the future."

"So you believe bullies can change."

"Some can. Some never do. You see it every day, in politics and business, on television. People who seize on the weakness of others, who are cruel in order to make themselves feel better." She set her half-empty glass on the kitchen counter behind her. "What makes a person decide to become a cop? I would think it would be a dangerous, often unpleasant job."

Was she equating cops with bullies? Or just trying to change the subject? "I'd hate sitting in an office," he said. "I liked solving problems and helping others. People don't always believe that, but most cops do." He drained his glass, then set it aside. "What makes a person want to teach preschool? It may not be dangerous, but I'm pretty sure it's unpleasant at times."

"Oh, very unpleasant," she agreed. "We still have children in diapers. And stomach flu season is always fun."

She laughed at the horror that must have shown on his face. "Don't tell me you'd rather face down bullets than a dirty diaper."

"Can I have another choice?"

"You're going to make a great dad someday."

"I hear it's different when it's your own kid."

"And I've heard that's a lie."

"Then I guess I'll learn to live with the disappointment."

Her eyes met his, and he felt that *zing!* of heat again. This was such an ordinary conversation, in a sunlit kitchen on a late spring afternoon, nothing stronger than water at hand, and yet it felt intimate, as if they were confiding deep secrets.

The doorbell rang, the chime overly loud in the stillness. "Are you expecting someone?" he asked.

"No."

He followed her to the front door. A woman dressed all in brown, like a UPS delivery person, but without the brown truck, stood on the top step. "Are you Audra Trask?" she asked Audra.

"Yes."

"This is for you." The woman pressed a large white envelope into Audra's hands. "You're being sued. All the details are in that packet." Not waiting for a response, the woman turned and walked away.

Audra held the envelope by the edges, staring at it as if afraid it might bite. Hud eased it from her hands. Audra's name and address were neatly typed on the label affixed to the front, but there was no return address. "Do you want me to open it?" he asked.

She shook her head and took the envelope from him, then tore open one end. She pulled out the papers and studied them. He leaned closer and read the ten-point legalese.

"Terrell, Davis and Compton are suing me," she said. "Me and my father. For fraud and libel and misappropriation of funds, and a lot of other legal terms I'm too stunned to make sense of right now." She shoved the papers back into the envelope. "Or ever. None of this makes sense. If my father did all the things they said he did, then fine, sue him. But I didn't have anything to do with any of it."

"Let me see that." He held out his hand, and she gave him the envelope. He read through the papers. "I'm not an attorney, but it appears to me they're saying you have knowledge of your father's dealings that you refuse to divulge. They're suing, I think, in an attempt to get you to tell what you know."

"I don't know anything," she said. "Why does TDC think I do?"

"I don't know." Was this an especially bold gambit on TDC's part, or merely a desperate one?

"Maybe this isn't about what TDC wants you to reveal," he said. "Maybe it's about what they think you know that they *don't* want you to say."

She pushed her hair back from her forehead, a

distracted gesture. "I don't understand what you're getting at."

"Everything TDC is doing—the charges against your father, the big reward, the publicity—those are the actions of an organization that is desperate to find your father."

"Because they want to stop him from talking?"

"I could be wrong, but I think so."

Most of the color had left her face, but she remained strong. "That sounds dangerous," she said. "A lot more dangerous than diapers."

"You don't have any idea what TDC might be worried about?" he asked. "It could even be something your father mentioned to you in passing."

"He didn't talk to me about his work. He knew I wasn't interested."

"What did you talk about?" Maybe the answer lay there.

"What I was doing. What was going on in my life." She shrugged. "Sometimes we talked about music, or movies, or books. Travel—that was something we both enjoyed. There was nothing secret or mysterious or having anything to do with TDC."

"If you think of anything else, call me." It was what he always said to people involved in cases, but he hoped she really would call him.

"I will." Did he detect annoyance in her voice?

"What will you do about the lawsuit?" he asked.

She looked down at the white envelope. "I'll contact my attorney. The whole thing is ridiculous. And annoying." She shifted her gaze to him at the last word. Maybe a signal for him to go.

"I'll let you know if I hear any news," he said, moving toward the door.

"Thanks."

"Try not to worry," he said, then added, "I'll protect you." Because it was the right thing to say. Because it was his job.

Because he realized nothing was more important to him at this moment.

Chapter Four

Audra was eating breakfast the next morning when her doorbell rang again. Heart in her throat, she tiptoed to the door, half expecting to see the brown-suited woman again, delivering another sheaf of dire-sounding legal documents. The first set sat on a table by the door. Audra would need to contact her attorney about them, but for now she was treating them like something contagious.

The man who stood on the steps wore a dull green windbreaker, jeans and dark blue athletic shoes, and had sandy blond hair that hung past his shoulders. He smiled at the peephole. "Is this Audra Trask's place—the woman who runs Canyon Critters Daycare? I'm sorry to bother you at home, but this was the only time I could see you."

A parent, she decided, relief flooding her. She undid the chain and opened the door. "What can I do for you?" she asked. "Do you have a child at Canyon Critters?"

"It's Roy," he said. "Roy Holliday. Can I come in?"

The name sounded familiar. Maybe he had recently put in an application. She opened the door a little wider. "If this is about a new admission, I'm afraid we won't have any new openings until we move into our new facility this fall."

He slipped past her, into the house. "Excuse me," she said, flustered by the move. "What is it you want?"

"You have the contract for the space next to the new elementary school, don't you?" he asked.

"That's right. Is this about a new enrollment?"

"Not exactly." He looked around her small home as if he were taking notes.

"Then why are you here?" she asked.

"Did your father help you get the contract at the new school?" he asked. "Since TDC is building that facility and he worked for them?"

"My father? Who are you? Why are you here?" She grabbed her phone off the table by the door. "You need to leave or I'm calling the police."

"You invited me in," he said. "You can't call the police."

"Oh, yes, I can." Hands shaking, she dialed 911.

He took the phone from her. "Don't do that."

She ran into the kitchen. He followed, not running, but walking fast enough to catch up. By the time he reached her, she stood on the other side of the room, a large chef's knife in her hands. "Oh, don't be like that!" he protested. "I just want to talk to you. I'm a reporter. I'm working on a story about your father."

"I don't want to talk to you," she said. "You need to leave."

Instead of leaving, he leaned back against the

counter and took out a notebook. "What was it like, growing up as Dane Trask's daughter?" he asked. "Did he take you hiking in Black Canyon National Park with him? Did you have any idea he was planning to disappear this way?"

"Leave!" she shouted. What had he done with her phone?

He ignored her, scribbling in his notebook. He studied the pictures on her refrigerator. "Hey, is this you, with your dad?" He plucked a photograph from beneath a magnet, one that showed her and her dad together two Christmases ago.

"Put that back!" she said.

He laid the photograph on the counter, pulled out his phone, took a picture, then turned back to her. "You don't look that much like your dad. I assume you take after your mother. What was she like? How did it feel, knowing your parents never married?"

Audra looked at the knife in her hand. She might defend herself with it, but she wasn't going to walk up and stab this guy—even if that might be the only way to make him leave. He was twice her size, so she couldn't shove him out the door. He clearly wasn't afraid of her.

If he wouldn't leave, she would. She walked out of the room and collected her purse and briefcase from the table by the sofa. She found her phone on the back of the sofa, but instead of dialing 911, she punched in Mark Hudson's number. "There is a man here who says he's a reporter and he refuses to leave," she said. "He says his name is Roy Holliday."

"What's he doing?" Mark asked.

"He's standing in my kitchen, making notes."

"Are you okay?"

"I'm really annoyed. If I opened the pantry and started throwing cans of soup at the guy, would that really count as assault? I think that might persuade him to leave."

"Don't do anything. If you're uncomfortable, go out and sit in your car with the doors locked."

"I'm not going to leave him alone to wander around my house at will," she said.

"I'm on my way."

He ended the call, and she tucked the phone in her pocket and headed back to the kitchen. "Mr. Holliday!" she called. "You had better not be snooping in my cabinets."

But Holliday was gone. The back door stood open, and the only other sign that he had been there was the photograph of her and her father, lying on the counter by the refrigerator.

HUD RAN HOT all the way into Montrose, lights and sirens clearing his path down the highway. When he hit the city limits, he slowed and shut off the fireworks, aware that he was no longer in his jurisdiction. Better not to alarm the locals, unless he needed their help.

He parked at the curb in front of Audra's house, and she met him at the front door. "He's gone," she said. "When I got off the phone with you, he wasn't there. The back door was open, so I guess he went out that way."

"How did he get into the house?" Hud asked.

She flushed. "I let him in, sort of. I was holding the door open to talk to him and he just slipped past. He caught me off guard. I thought he was a parent wanting to talk about enrolling a child in school. I mean, I jumped to conclusions, but he let me believe them."

"Audra!"

"I know, I know. It was very stupid of me. But he looked so harmless. And he was, I guess." She led the way back into the house. "I tried to call you back and let you know you didn't need to come all the way out here, but your phone went to voice mail."

"I was driving."

"Oh. Right."

"What did he do while he was here?" Hud asked.

"He looked around. He asked a lot of questions about my dad. I didn't answer them. He took a picture of a photograph of the two of us that I had on my refrigerator." She rubbed her shoulders. "It was calm and kind of ridiculous and really creepy, too."

"Don't let anyone else inside who you don't know," Hud said.

She nodded. "I know. It's just—this whole situation is so bizarre. My father, the lawsuit and everything."

"Have you talked to anyone about that lawsuit?" he asked.

"I have an appointment with my lawyer this afternoon." She checked her watch. "And I really have to go. Thank you for rushing all the way out here."

"I never mind an excuse to see you." He turned

toward her. "You could make it up to me by having dinner with me tonight."

That blush again, her cheeks rose pink, her eyes bright. "Officer Hudson, are you sure…"

"Like I said before, call me Hud. Everyone does."

"All right. Hud. Are you sure it's, well, ethical to get involved with someone who's part of a case you're working on?"

"You're not a suspect or even a witness to a crime. You're the daughter of a missing person we're searching for."

"That's all my father is to you—a missing person? Not a desperate fugitive or a fleeing criminal or any of the other descriptions I've seen on the news?"

"He's a man who went missing in our jurisdiction, so we're trying to find him." He also might be a fugitive and a criminal, but they didn't know that yet. There were a great many rumors circulating about Dane Trask, but thus far Hud had seen very little proof of anything truly criminal about the man.

"Thank you for saying that, even if it's not true."

"Does that mean you'll have dinner with me?"

"I'll think about it."

He'd have to be satisfied. She picked up her purse and briefcase. "I'll walk out with you."

She locked the door behind him, then he followed her to her car. As she opened the driver's-side door of the black RAV4, she froze. "I know that wasn't there last night," she said.

Hud moved around her to examine the note tucked under the driver's side windshield wiper. He slipped on a pair of gloves, then carefully lifted the note from beneath the wiper blade and spread it out on the hood of the car. Audra leaned in beside him, pressed against him as they read.

You need to be careful who you talk to, or you'll be next.

"THE NEXT WHAT?" Audra asked for the third time as she sat across a table from Hud, Officer Beck and a woman who introduced herself at Officer Redhorse at the Ranger Brigade headquarters. Reluctantly, she had agreed to come here and give her statement before going into work. She had telephoned Brenda and let her know she would be late, though she had avoided her assistant's attempts to find out why.

"The next person hurt?" Officer Redhorse suggested.

"The next person to disappear?" Beck offered.

"You're not making me feel any better about this," Audra said.

No one pointed out that it wasn't their job to make her feel better, so she was grateful for that, at least. Hud was trying to soothe her frazzled nerves. She remembered him saying he had become a cop because he wanted to help. She was beginning to believe that. "Could Roy Holliday have left that note?" he asked.

"Why would he?" she asked. "He got into my house and was talking to me. He didn't even have to threaten me to get me to let him in." The more she thought about the way she'd behaved with the reporter, the more like an idiot she felt.

"Maybe he wasn't sure he'd get you to let him in, so he left the note before he rang your doorbell," Beck said. "Did you see where he was parked?"

"No." She paused, trying to re-create the scene in her head. "I looked out the peephole and he was standing on the steps. He apologized for coming to my house so early and said he needed to talk to me. I asked if it was about a student and he didn't say no."

"You say he left out the back door," Officer Red-horse said.

"When I returned to the kitchen, the back door was open and he was gone," she said. "I didn't actually see him leave."

"Did you hear him leave?" Beck asked.

"No. I was on the phone with Hud—with Officer Hudson. I wasn't listening." She should have been listening. What if he had tried to sneak up behind her? "Why don't you call him and ask him about the note?" she asked. "If he's a reporter, you should be able to get in touch with him."

"He hasn't answered my calls," Hud said. "I left a message."

"He probably thinks you're going to give him a hard time about being at my house," she said. "He won't call back."

"Who else would threaten you?" she asked.

"No one," Audra said. "I run a day care center. I don't make enemies."

"You have employees," Beck said. "Are any of them upset with you? Are any parents angry?"

She thought of Jana, who resented taking direction from a younger woman. But Jana was a good, dedicated teacher. In her shoes, Audra might feel the same. Jana had had a successful day care of her own that she had had to give up when her husband transferred. Now she was working for a much younger woman, used to making her own decisions but unable to do so. So yes, Jana resented Audra, but why make dire threats against her?

As for parents, April's mother wasn't happy at how her child's bullying had been dealt with, but Mrs. Patrick struck Audra as being as gentle and harmless as her little girl. "I can't think of anyone," she said. "Truly."

"You don't recognize the handwriting?" Redhorse asked.

"It's just block printing. No, I don't recognize it."

"What about the paper?" Beck asked.

"It looks like a sheet of plain copy paper." She shook her head. "Maybe this is someone's idea of a sick joke. I mean, that threat is so vague. It doesn't say what is going to happen or who I'm not supposed to talk to or give me any idea what I'm not supposed to say."

"TDC Enterprises sued you," Hud said. "They think you know something your father also knows."

She had tossed and turned half the night, trying to make sense of that lawsuit. "The papers I was given don't say that," she said.

"No, but it's implied," Hud said.

"But why would someone from TDC leave a note

on my car?" she asked. "I think they sent a clear enough message with the lawsuit." She shook her head. "The more I consider this, the more I think this is just a bad joke." She frowned at the piece of paper.

"Has anyone from TDC contacted you since your father disappeared?" Redhorse asked.

"No."

"Does that surprise you?" Redhorse asked.

"Not really. I hardly knew anyone at that office. And I'm baffled as to why they're dragging me into this lawsuit. There's absolutely nothing I can tell them."

They all fell silent. "Any other questions?" Hud asked.

"No," Redhorse said. "Thank you for coming in."

"Yeah, thanks," Beck said. They all stood.

"I'll walk you out," Hud said.

He didn't say anything else until they stood by her car. "Are you okay?" he asked. "This kind of thing can really shake a person up."

"I'm okay," she said. "I guess I don't scare so easy. It seems more ridiculous to me than anything— that silly confrontation with that reporter, then this vaguely threatening note. It's ludicrous."

"Are you sure? Do you want me to come sleep on your couch tonight?"

She didn't know whether to be flattered or amused by the offer. There was definitely some attraction be- tween them—she'd felt it at their very first meeting, right after she had learned of her father's disappearance. Sometimes, it almost felt as if he was coming on to her. Other times, she was sure he saw her as just another link to her father, a man he was trying to find. "That won't be necessary. I'm fine, really." She unlocked the car and opened her door, deciding as she did so that now was as good a time as any to clarify where she stood with this man. "But I will take you up on your other offer."

"What offer is that?" he asked.

"I'll go to dinner with you."

When he grinned, he was even more handsome. "When?"

"Why not tonight? Then you can take me home and see for yourself that everything is just fine."

"It's a date."

"Good." And if someone happened to be lurking around, it wouldn't hurt for them to see that she had a capable cop in her corner.

CHERYL ARNOTTE HAD hair the red-brown of pine bark and intense gray eyes. She also had a little girl and a little boy who attended Canyon Critters, and a reputation as a good civil attorney. From time to time, she handled legal matters for the day care center and had agreed to meet with Audra Wednesday afternoon. "While I'll want more time to review this completely, I can see two motives for this suit," Arnotte said after the two women had visited briefly. "One, they're hoping word gets back to your father that they've involved you and he'll come out of hiding in order to protect you. Or two, they think you have money or information or something that this suit will bring into the open."

"The Ranger Brigade think TDC is digging for information they believe my father shared with me," Audra said. "He didn't tell me anything, but maybe someone thinks he did. In any case, whatever sent my father into hiding, I doubt he'll come out just to protect me from an annoying and baseless lawsuit."

"Even baseless suits can be time-consuming and expensive," Arnotte said. "If we're unlucky and can't find a judge to dismiss this, this could drag on for a very long time."

"I have to fight them," Audra said. "I don't have a choice."

"All right. Then I'll proceed. Have you spoken to anyone at TDC about this?"

"No."

"Don't. If anyone tries to contact you, refer them to me."

Audra signed papers, wrote out a check and left the office, feeling drained. She debated calling and canceling her date with Hud, but that would leave her home alone all evening to brood, and that thought was even more depressing.

At home, she was changing clothes when she heard a car door slam. She checked the clock: six forty-five. She and Hud had agreed to meet at seven. She gave him credit for being eager, but they'd have to have a talk about why it wasn't a good idea to show up before your date had time to get ready. She cinched on her robe and went to the front window and peered out.

The sun had just dipped behind the roofs of the houses across the street, casting her side into deep shadow, but it was still light enough to see there was no one parked at the curb. Angling her head, she spotted a dark shape behind her car, blending into the shadow cast by a tall pine. Maybe Hud had realized he was too early and was sitting out there now. She started to open the door and call out to him, but remembering her earlier mistake with the reporter, pulled out her phone instead.

Are you sitting in my driveway? she texted.

No answer. She watched the car in her driveway. The shape didn't look like a Ranger Brigade cruiser, but then, Hud would probably bring his personal vehicle, wouldn't he?

The crunch of gravel made her jump. Was that footsteps? Every hair on the back of her neck stood on end, and she shrank from the window.

Her phone pinged. I'm on my way there. About ten minutes out.

Hurry! she answered.

The phone vibrated in her hand. She scrambled to silence it and retreated into the kitchen, searching for the same knife she'd used to defend herself against Roy Holliday. "Audra, what's going on?" Hud asked when she answered.

"There's a car parked behind mine in the driveway." She spoke softly, just above a whisper. "At least,

I think it's a car. It's really dark over there, so I can't tell much. But I was in the bedroom getting dressed and I thought I heard a car door. I thought you were here early."

"Call 911," he said. "Now. I'll be there as soon as I can."

Chapter Five

Audra dialed 911, gave her name and address to the dispatcher, and explained what was going on. "We'll send a car right over," the man on the other end of the phone said.

He offered to stay on the line with her, but she declined, instead pocketing the phone, then tiptoeing through the house, double-checking the locks on all the doors and windows. That took two minutes. Another seven before Hud would be here. She didn't want to look out the window, but she couldn't stop herself. The vehicle was still there, a bulky shadow crouched behind her RAV4, menacing in its indistinctness.

She carried a kitchen chair into the hall and sat where she had a view of both doors, but she doubted anyone could see her. She leaned forward, straining to catch any sound, and thought she heard a scraping like a shoe on concrete.

Then lights lit up the front of the house. Heart pounding, she jumped up, almost knocking over the chair. Men shouted and feet pounded against pavement. Car doors slammed, followed by a racing engine and the squeal of tires. She reached the front window in time to see a Montrose Police Department cruiser speeding away.

A second patrol car pulled to the curb, followed by a dark pickup. The vehicles parked, and Hud emerged from the truck, a familiar, comforting figure. She opened the door as Hud and two Montrose police officers approached her. "Are you all right?" Hud called when he was halfway up the walk.

"I'm fine."

"Ma'am, would you put the knife away, please?" one of the officers said.

She stared down at the knife in her hand. She'd forgotten she had it. "Sorry," she mumbled, and laid the knife on the hall table.

Hud walked up and embraced her. She hadn't realized how much she needed that embrace until his strong arms encircled her. She wanted to bury her face against his shoulder and stay there until her heartbeat slowed and this panicked feeling subsided.

But she was acutely aware of the two police officers standing in front of her, so she remained standing straight and faced them. "Thank you for getting here so quickly," she said.

"We have a unit in pursuit of your trespasser," said the older of the two officers, gray at the temples of his curly black hair and lines etched deeply in his mahogany skin. "Can you give us a description of the vehicle or the person driving it?"

She shook her head. "I'm sorry, I can't. It was

parked over there, in the shadow of that tree." She indicated the spot. "I had the impression it was dark and fairly large, like a larger SUV. Bigger than my RAV4. And I never saw the driver. I only heard footsteps outside."

The officer's radio crackled and a voice announced they had lost the vehicle they were pursuing. "We'll search the area for shoe impressions and other evidence," the younger officer, red-haired and freckled, said.

Only after they left did Audra remember she was wearing just her bathrobe and underwear, her feet bare and her hair uncombed. "I should get dressed," she said, pulling the robe more tightly around her.

"All right," Hud said. "I'll wait in the living room."

Instead of the dress she had planned to wear for their date, she pulled on leggings and a long T-shirt. Clothes that were comfortable and comforting. When she walked into the living room, she found Hud standing before her bookshelf, studying the titles there. "Do you like to read?" she asked.

"I do." He tapped the spine of a J. D. Robb novel. "I love this series," he said.

"Yeah. Me, too."

They talked about books for a while, and she began to feel calmer. Then the two Montrose officers returned, and Hud sat beside Audra on the sofa while she gave her statement to the officers. After they left, he gathered her close and held her for a long moment, not saying anything. "I'm all right," she said after a while, and sat up straight. "Really. But I don't know if I'm up to going out for dinner."

"How about we order a pizza?" he suggested.

"That sounds perfect."

"Do you want to get a bottle of wine to go with it?" he asked.

"No, thanks. I'm not much of a drinker. I have some sparkling water and some sodas."

"A soda sounds great."

She appreciated that he didn't question her decision not to drink. It had been a problem with other men she dated. It had become a kind of test for her—if he objected too much, she knew he wasn't the man for her.

When the pizza arrived, they sat on the floor in front of the coffee table and ate. Audra began to relax. Hud wasn't in uniform tonight. He wore gray cargo pants and a blue T-shirt and light casual jacket. She could almost forget he was a cop. It helped that he didn't ask her more about what happened tonight. She had gone over everything with the Montrose police and didn't want to relive those frightening moments anymore.

"How did it go today with the lawyer?" he asked instead.

"It went okay. She thinks we have a good chance of getting the suit dismissed." She licked pizza sauce from her fingers. "She thinks TDC may have filed the suit to try to draw out Dad. They think he'll come out of hiding in order to protect me."

"Do you think that will work?"

"No. If he hears about it he'll be angry. And maybe

even a little worried. But he taught me to stand on my own two feet." She wiped her hands and tossed the paper napkin beside the remains of the pizza. "And he knows I don't need protection against a nuisance lawsuit."

Hud moved closer. He wasn't much older than her, she guessed, but he had fine lines at the corners of his eyes and the weathered skin of a man who spent a lot of time outdoors. If you didn't know what he did for a living, you might mistake him for a surfer or a snowboarder. "There are other things you might need protection against," he said.

"Oh? Like cops with big guns?" She shifted her gaze to his biceps, which stretched the fabric of his shirt.

"I was thinking of whoever was sneaking around out there tonight."

She looked away. She should have known they couldn't stay away from this topic for long. "Maybe it was that reporter."

"Maybe. But he walked right up to you before. Why not do that again?"

"Because I know him now. He knows I wouldn't let him in."

"I've been watching the news. I haven't seen any more reports from him."

"He said he was working on a story about my dad. That could be a pretty complex story at this point. Dad has been away weeks now, and there are all kinds of wild rumors flying around about him."

He rubbed her back, gently, the heat of his palm

penetrating the thin fabric of the T-shirt. "I'm worried about you here alone."

She resisted the urge to lean into his touch and straightened her spine. "I have good locks and a cell phone. And I know not to open the door to strangers, even friendly looking strangers. That's why I called you tonight, instead of stepping outside to see who was there. At this point, I wouldn't open the door for a Girl Scout selling cookies."

He took his hand away. "Are you sure you're only twenty-three? Because you sure have it more together than I did when I was twenty-three."

"How do you know I'm only twenty-three?" He made her sound impossibly young.

"I know everything about you." He shrugged. "Well, everything that's part of the public record."

"Most people just google their dates," she said.

His smile took some of the sting out of his words. "Cops go the extra mile."

"Hmm." She wasn't sure how she felt about that. He probably knew about the traffic ticket she got for speeding in a school zone when she was sixteen, but he clearly didn't know everything.

"Did you google me?" he asked.

She shook her head. "Only because I haven't had time." She tilted her head, considering him. "How old are you?"

"I'm twenty-eight."

"Oh, an old man. Wise in the ways of the world."

"A law enforcement career has a way of maturing a person in a hurry."

"Is that another way of saying you're jaded?"

"We weren't talking about me, we were talking about you." He leaned toward her, not touching, but close enough she could sense the heat from his body and distinguish individual golden eyelashes. "Are you just naturally precocious? I'll bet there aren't many twenty-three-year-olds with their own successful businesses."

"And I think that's a bet you'd lose. Let's just say my parents encouraged independence." She had lived a lot in her twenty-three years, not all of it good, but all of it part of who she was today. She stifled a yawn.

"Is that a not-so-subtle way of telling me it's time for me to go home?" Not waiting for an answer, he heaved himself to his feet and began clearing the remains of the pizza.

"It's been a long couple of days," she said. "But thanks for coming over. And thanks for the pizza."

"I'll leave, but don't be alarmed if you see my car circle the block a couple of times. I just want to make sure the coast is clear."

"I feel safer already."

She kissed him goodbye at the door, a deep, languid kiss that set every nerve tingling and could have led to more, if she had let it. But she pulled away, smiling, savoring the delicious tension and tantalizing anticipation, like an enthralling novel whose last page read "to be continued…"

IN THE FOLLOWING DAYS, Hud knew he was falling for Audra. All the signs were there—the intense focus on her when they were together, the desire to know everything about her and most of all the difficulty of keeping her out of his thoughts. He'd be compiling a spreadsheet of evidence in a case and find his mind wandering to an image of her slim figure, clad only in her bathrobe. Or he'd be studying footage of a crime scene and find himself thinking about something amusing she had said, or a joke he wanted to share with her later. The distractions were maddening, yet he didn't want them to stop. He wondered if she thought about him even half as much.

She probably didn't. She seemed to enjoy their time together, but he sensed she was holding back. She had secrets—some pain in her past she wasn't yet ready to reveal. She didn't know yet how patient he could be. When she was ready to open up to him, he'd be there, willing to hear what she had to say and to give whatever she needed.

Friday, two days after Montrose police responded to the call at Audra's house, Detective Marty Burns contacted Hud. "We caught the man who was snooping around your girlfriend's house," Burns said. "You want to observe while we question him?"

Hud didn't correct Burns's assumption that Audra was his girlfriend. "Thanks. I'd like that."

So it was that an hour later, Hud stood behind a one-way mirror, looking in on a gray-walled interrogation room at the Montrose Police Department at a slight man with close-cropped white hair and a soul patch, who fidgeted restlessly as he sat alone at a metal table that was bolted to the floor. "The officer who pursued him got a partial license plate and the make and model of the vehicle, and we were able to track him down that way," explained Detective Burns, who had the heavy jowls and thick body of a man who worked too many hours and ate too much fast food. "His name is Richard Salazar, and he's a private detective."

He left Hud alone behind the mirror and went to question Salazar. After the preliminaries for the recording, Burns got down to business. "What were you doing parked in the driveway of 122 Zane Court on the evening of June 3?" he asked.

"I wanted to talk to the woman who lives in the house." Salazar's tone was dismissive, annoyed that the police were wasting his time this way. "I knocked, but she didn't answer my knock. I was on my way back to my car when the police showed up, hit me with a spotlight and started yelling like I was an ax murderer or something."

"Do you know the woman who lives in that house?" Burns asked.

"Audra Trask. I've never met her before. I wanted to talk to her on behalf of a client."

"Who's your client?"

Salazar smirked. "That information is confidential."

Burns remained impassive. "Ms. Trask says you never knocked on her door, and you didn't ring the bell."

"She must not have heard me."

"She telephoned the dispatcher at 6:47 to report a strange car parked in her driveway. The first officer arrived on the scene at 6:56 and spotted you at the corner of the house, some fifteen feet from the front door. What were you doing for the nine minutes between the time Ms. Trask saw your vehicle and the time police arrived?"

"I was looking around."

"Were you looking for a way into the house? An unlocked window or a door you could force?"

Salazar frowned. "I'm a private detective, not a thief."

"You were trespassing," Burns said. "I could have your license revoked for that."

"I was doing my job."

"You were a stranger to Ms. Trask, prowling around her yard in the dark when you weren't authorized to be there. Ms. Trask is prepared to press charges for trespassing."

"I was doing my job," Salazar said, louder this time.

"Why did you run when the patrol car showed up?" Burns asked.

"I was afraid. The way they were shouting and carrying on, I figured they were going to shoot me. That happens all the time these days."

Burns looked wearier than ever. "Try again. Why did you run?"

"I told you, I was scared."

"You were scared we'd find the baggie of heroin stuffed under the front seat of your vehicle," Burns said.

Salazar drew back as if slapped. "I don't know what you're talking about!"

Burns stood and leaned over the table, his face

close to Salazar's. "Who hired you to 'investigate' Ms. Trask?"

Salazar remained mute.

"I'll be contacting the state licensing board as soon as I leave this room," Burns said. "And recommending no bail on the drug charges."

"I was hired by a guy named Lawrence," Salazar said. "That's all I know. He paid cash, and there's an email I'm supposed to send my report to."

"Is Lawrence his first name or last name?"

"I don't know. He just said to call him Lawrence."

"What did he look like?"

"I never saw him. He called me and sent the money via PayPal."

"You didn't think that was unusual? Maybe even illegal?" Burns asked.

"There was nothing illegal about it. And some people don't want other people to know they hired me. Divorce cases, for example." He shrugged. "He paid cash and didn't argue about the price."

"What did he want to know about Ms. Trask?" Burns asked.

"He just said he wanted me to find out everything I could about Audra Trask."

"Why?"

"He didn't tell me his reasons, and I didn't ask."

"What did you find out?"

"Enough." Salazar sat back. "And that's all I'm going to stay. You may think my standards aren't very high, but I have some."

Burns looked at him for a moment, then left the

room. Another officer entered and escorted Salazar away. "Any ideas on who hired him?" Burns asked Hud when he rejoined him.

"TDC Enterprises has filed a bogus lawsuit against her and her father," Hud said. "Maybe they wanted to do some anonymous snooping."

"Her dad is Dane Trask, right? The guy loose in the national park?"

"Yeah. It's a tough situation for her."

"If we find out anything else, I'll let you know," Burns said. "Do you want to notify Ms. Trask, or should we?"

"Let me do it," Hud said. He didn't like being the bearer of bad news, but Audra had proved she wasn't easily shaken.

SHAKEN WAS NOT the word Audra would have used to describe how she felt when Hud told her about Richard Salazar and the mysterious "Lawrence." "Forget the kitchen knife," she raged, pacing back and forth across her kitchen in agitation. "If that man shows up here again, I'll brain him with my cast-iron frying pan. How dare he!"

"That man will be in prison for the next little while," Hud said. "The Montrose cops found heroin in his car when they arrested him."

Some of the anger leaked away, replaced by a pang of sympathy. "He probably bought it with whatever Lawrence paid him," she said. "Maybe prison will be a good thing. Maybe it will help him kick the habit."

"Maybe." She felt Hud's gaze on her, full of questions, so she changed the subject. "I haven't heard anything from my lawyer yet. I called her office and left a message, but I haven't heard back."

"People talk about swift justice, but in my experience the process usually takes time," he said. "You should tell your lawyer about Salazar and Lawrence, though. There might be a connection to TDC."

"You mean 'Lawrence' might be someone with TDC, trying to dig up dirt on me?"

"I can't imagine what kind of dirt he thinks he'll get on a woman who runs a day care center." Hud kissed her cheek. "I have to go. I just stopped by for a minute to give you the news."

"Thanks."

After Hud left, Audra continued to pace her office. Usually when she struggled with something like this, she called her father for advice. He had a knack for listening, asking questions and helping her plot the right course. Unlike her mother and various girlfriends she might have confided in, her father had no patience with avoiding confrontation or sitting around hoping things would resolve without her intervention. "Problems seldom get better if allowed to fester," he said. "If you want a solution, you have to tackle the issue head-on. Fighting is better than fidgeting any day of the week."

She took out her phone and called Cheryl Arnotte's office again. A pleasant female voice invited her to leave a message. She ended the call without leaving a message, then stared at the photograph of her and her father that sat on the credenza behind her desk.

"If you knew you were going to leave, you might have left something more useful behind," she said. "A letter or a diary, or some explanation for all of this."

She still loved her father, but right now, she had never felt more abandoned.

Chapter Six

"The Park Service reports that Dane Trask sightings have dwindled to only three in the past two weeks." Ranger Brigade commander Grant Sanderlin addressed his officers at Monday morning roll call. The FBI special agent had assumed command of the Rangers only a few weeks before Trask's disappearance, and it seemed to Hud that the frustrations of the case had added a few more strands of silver to Sanderlin's sandy hair.

"How many confirmed sightings?" second-in-command Lieutenant Michael Dance asked. A veteran with the Rangers, Dance had deep shadows beneath his dark eyes these days, a testimony to sleepless nights as father to a new baby girl.

"No confirmed sightings," Sanderlin said.

"He's been quiet since that attack on Braxton," Rand Knightbridge said. Knightbridge, along with his Belgian Malinois, Lotte, were an expert tracking team, though they had had no luck locating the elusive Dane Trask. "Maybe he's moved on."

"Maybe." The commander sounded doubtful.

"Maybe he's dead," Ethan Reynolds said. A man who listened more than he spoke, Ethan studied psychology and talked of one day becoming a profiler. His talents had come in useful more than once for the Rangers.

Hud hoped for Audra's sake her father was still alive, but death was a definite possibility. The wilderness where Trask had chosen to hole up was filled with hidden canyons, steep drop-offs and miles of roadless backcountry. A minor slip that resulted in a broken bone could be deadly for a man alone.

"If he's still out there, I don't think he'll remain quiet for too much longer," Sanderlin said. "All of his communications to this point have made some kind of accusation against TDC Enterprises, to little effect. He wants something, and I think he'll keep agitating until he gets it."

"TDC's big reward hasn't gotten any results yet," Jason Beck observed. "They may make a new move soon, too."

Hud thought of the lawsuit TDC had filed against Audra and her father. He had reported the lawsuit at an earlier meeting. If TDC had hoped to draw out Trask with the suit, they hadn't succeeded. Hud wasn't sure how Trask did it, but he seemed to keep up with the news. Did he have a volunteer on the outside who was funneling updates and supplies to him? Audra would be the most likely candidate, but Hud believed her assertion that she hadn't been in touch with her father.

"Officer Hudson, did you hear me?"

Hud started, and his face heated. "Sorry, sir. I was thinking."

"Stop, before you hurt yourself," Beck quipped.

"The Forest Service has hired a contractor to clear the illegal construction dump site in Curecanti Recreation Area," Sanderlin said. "They're going to start work tomorrow. I want someone on-site in case they turn up anything new. Beck will take the morning shift—you can relieve him at noon."

"We've combed through all that like it was an archaeological dig," Dance said. "We came up with nada."

"We have a child's drawing, a man's work glove and a key to a standard padlock," Reynolds corrected. These items had been dutifully tested, tagged, bagged and placed in the Rangers' evidence lockers, but had yielded no information that pointed to who had dumped hundreds of yards of construction debris in the middle of the wilderness.

"The Forest Service is anxious to get it cleared out," Sanderlin continued. "We'll continue to run regular patrols out that way for the next few months, in case the original dumpers decide to try again."

"It's not like there aren't miles of other places they can use as their free disposal site," Redhorse said. "People do it all the time."

"Yeah, but they dump a single refrigerator or a television set," Knightbridge said. "Maybe a junked car. It took weeks, and truckload after truckload, to dump everything at that site."

"And they did it right under our noses," Hud said. That grated more than anything.

"The Forest Service has submitted a proposal for drone patrols to monitor wildlife populations," Sanderlin said. "But they could also look for illegal dump sites like this one. If funding is approved, it has the potential to curtail problems like this one."

"Maybe the drone can find Dane Trask," Knightbridge said. "He can't hide from the eye in the sky."

Hud wasn't so sure about that. Trask operated by his own rules, and Hud was beginning to believe the man wouldn't be found until he was ready to reveal himself.

THE ARREST OF twelve people in a local burglary ring dominated the papers and television news, so for the next couple of days no stories about Dane Trask appeared. He didn't leave any more mysterious messages or tangle with any hikers, and while Audra continued to worry about him, she was glad he wasn't causing more trouble.

She began to relax a little, to focus on her job and her growing relationship with Mark Hudson. She thought her dad would probably like him. Dane invariably intimidated her dates—a former army ranger who could still run rings around men twenty years his junior could do that. But she thought Hud wasn't the type to be easily intimidated. The idea pleased her.

But life wasn't all romance and optimism. Monday morning brought an unwelcome phone call. "Ms. Trask, Superintendent Wells would like to see you in his office at ten thirty." The woman on the other end of the line didn't identify herself, but she didn't have to. Audra recognized the voice of the woman who was the assistant to school superintendent Vernon Wells.

"Why does he want to see me?" Audra asked.

"I'm sure I don't know, but it's important. Can I tell him you'll be here?"

Audra thought of several things the assistant could tell the superintendent, but thought better of all of them. "Of course I'll be there."

Audra had just enough time to finish her coffee, comb her hair, freshen her lipstick and drive to the school district offices. The assistant—Maeve or Mavis or Madge or something like that—wore her customary smirk, sweeping a judging look over Audra's neat gray slacks and purple blouse, pausing in her survey to frown at the small stud in Audra's nose.

Mr. Wells didn't look happy to see her. A large man with abundant chins and thinning hair, he studied Audra from behind black-framed glasses. "What did you need to see me about?" Audra asked as she slid into the chair across from the superintendent's desk. Maybe he had a report on the construction project at the new school, or he needed her input about some furnishings for the day care center.

"I'm very concerned about the negative publicity surrounding you," he said.

Audra blinked. "I'm not aware of any negative publicity about *me*."

"There are wanted posters for your father all over

town. He's in the news constantly. I hear now he's attacked a hiker in the park and almost killed the man."

She couldn't believe that just when she thought public interest in her father was dying down, *this* happened. "My father is not me," she said. "You can't blame me for things he may or may not be doing."

"People see the name Trask and they associate it with bad things," he said.

"I have no control over what people think," she protested.

"Still, there are people who have suggested that we shouldn't have the Trask name associated with our new preschool and day care."

What people? she wanted to ask. But that was the kind of question people like Wells never answered. "My preschool and day care isn't a school facility," she said. "It's an independent business that happens to lease space from the school. It's an innovative model that will benefit parents, students, employees of nearby TDC Enterprises and teachers with children who will now have on-site day care." That was a direct quote from the bid she had submitted when she had first learned of the plans for the new buildings. A bid that had persuaded the school board to vote unanimously to award her the contract. "We have a contract," she added.

"The contract has a morals clause."

She flushed. "I haven't done anything immoral."

He shuffled papers on his desk, avoiding her gaze. "I wanted to extend you the courtesy of letting you know where the board's thinking is leading," he said.

"What do you expect me to do about it?"

"I don't know. But perhaps you could think of a way to separate yourself from your father. To demonstrate your fine character so that parents will feel comfortable trusting you with their children."

"Parents already feel comfortable trusting me with their children," she said. "My school is at full capacity."

"Maybe some testimonials from those parents would help," he said. "It's worth considering."

Audra had no memory of leaving the superintendent's office, or of the drive back to her school. Rage blotted out everything else—rage at Superintendent Wells for blaming her for her father's actions, closely followed by rage at her father for running away and acting like a wild man.

Maybe he really was ill, she thought. Maybe something in her dad had snapped, and that was why he was living in the wilderness doing inexplicable things. In that case, he needed to come home so she could help him. He definitely didn't need to be there, ruining her life from a distance.

By the time she pulled into the parking lot she had calmed down a little. She had a job to do, and she needed to focus on that and worry about the rest later. Walking down the hall toward her office, she spotted Jana Keplar and her class of four-year-olds filing into the lunchroom and detoured toward them.

When Audra took her seat at the end of the lunch table, Jana frowned at her. "Hello, Ms. Keplar," Audra said. "Hello, children."

"Are you going to eat lunch with us again today?" a little boy with a shaved head asked.

"I'm going to eat lunch with Mia today." Audra focused on Mia, a sturdy girl with long brown hair and hazel eyes.

Mia smiled back and bounced in her seat in excitement. "Do we get ice cream?" she asked.

"Yes, you do," Audra agreed.

"Can I have chocolate?" Mia asked as she walked beside Audra to the table in the corner. The staff had placed a vase of fresh flowers on the table, and Mrs. Garibaldi soon arrived with their sparkling water and ice cream—chocolate for Mia.

Audra had to spend a little time getting some of the children to relax and talk to her, but she didn't have to work at all with Mia. By the time Mia had eaten half of her turkey sandwich, she had told Audra about her baby brother; her dog, Sam, and her cat, Pumpkin; her ballet class; and her favorite subject—art. She smiled and laughed and was the picture of a sunny, friendly child.

Only when she stopped to eat her ice cream was Audra able to get a word in edgewise. "I especially wanted to have lunch with you today, Mia," she said, "because I think you can help me with something."

Mia's eyes widened. "Of course I'll help you, Ms. Trask."

"It's your classmate, April. I'm afraid she has a hard time making friends, and I'm hoping you'll be her friend."

Mia's bright smile faded. "I don't like April," she said.

"Why don't you like her?" Audra asked.

"She's such a crybaby. My baby brother cries less

than she does. I'm almost five and I never cry. At least, not about things that aren't important. I mean, you can't even look at her and she cries. Plus, she's a tattletale. If I so much as bump into her in line, she runs to tattle to Mrs. Keplar."

Audra listened to this outburst in dismay. From Mia's point of view, April's behavior did sound tiresome. She carefully considered her next words. "You're very lucky, Mia," she said. "You find it so easy to talk to people and to make friends. Not everyone is made that way. Some people are shyer. They don't know what to say to other people, and being in new situations frightens them."

"I am very lucky, Ms. Trask," Mia said, her face serious.

"I think April is shy," Audra said. "She doesn't know what to say, and maybe she's even afraid. It would help so much if you could be nice to her."

"I'm not mean to her," Mia protested. "She even called me a bully, and that wasn't right. That's calling names."

"It's calling names when you say she's a crybaby," Audra said gently.

Mia pressed her lips together. "Try to be April's friend," Audra said. "For me? I believe you could really help her."

"She can't be my best friend," Mia said. "That's Maddie Friar."

"April doesn't have to be your best friend. Just… try to say one nice thing to her every day."

Mia sighed with the drama only an almost-five-year-old can manage. "I can try," she said.

"Thank you." Audra held up her glass of sparkling water. "Let's drink a toast to that."

Mia grinned, and the two clinked glasses. Audra's mood lightened. This was why she had opened her day care center, not to please bureaucrats like Superintendent Wells, but to make a difference to children like Mia and April.

"WE'RE NOT UNCOVERING anything the crime scene team might have missed, but the men know to keep a lookout for anything that might identify who dumped all this." Officer Jason Beck had to shout to be heard over the roar of the front-end loader that was scooping up mounds of construction debris and depositing them in the back of a big dump truck when Hud arrived at the dump site Tuesday afternoon.

Hud nodded and squinted in the bright sunshine at the piles of old timbers, rock and gypsum board scattered across an acre of sagebrush scrub. An aerial search for Dane Trask a couple of weeks ago had discovered instead this illegal dump, located on federal land just outside of the national park boundary. "I talked to every major construction outfit in a hundred-mile radius," Beck said as the front-end loader moved farther away, making conversation more possible. "And some not-so-major ones. They all swear they had nothing to do with this. A lot of them offered to show me their dumping receipts for the last three months."

"The guilty party isn't likely to confess," Hud said. "And I bet dumping receipts can be faked easily enough."

"Whoever did this, they stopped as soon as we started watching the place," Beck said. "They're either really wary or really lucky."

"Maybe our patrols or the drone surveillance the Forest Service is proposing will help," Hud said.

"At least we can be pretty sure Dane Trask didn't have anything to do with this," Beck said. "As much as that man has been a thorn in our sides, at least there's that."

"He's like our own bigfoot, a boogeyman people can scare themselves with," Hud said. For a while there had been almost daily reports from hikers who had claimed to have seen Trask or been chased by him. Almost all of them had turned out to be either attempts to gain attention or people scaring themselves into seeing what wasn't there.

"Hey, I almost forgot to show you this." Beck pulled out his wallet and took something from it. "Cara brought this home yesterday. Someone was selling them at the bookstore downtown." He handed over what turned out to be an oval white decal, the words *Free Dane Trask* filling the oval.

"People can't decide if he's a criminal, a myth or a folk hero." Hud returned the decal, then both men turned as shouts rose from across the open ground. The man operating the front-end loader shut down the machine and leaned out of the cab, waving frantically.

Hud ran, Beck right behind him. The worker

pointed toward the front of his machine. A few steps from the bucket, Hud halted. A man's body lay half out of the debris, mouth open, one arm flung over his head, like a drowning man emerging from a tumultuous sea.

"He hasn't been there long," Beck said. He looked up into the bright blue sheet of sky. "No ravens circling."

"I just saw him last week." Hud took out his phone to summon help, then slipped it back into his pocket. No cell service out here. "That's Roy Holliday," he said. The reporter must have asked too many questions of the wrong person.

Chapter Seven

Audra arrived at her office after lunch Tuesday to find a Free Dane Trask sticker on her desk. Brenda came in and found her staring at it. "Who put this here?" Audra asked.

Brenda shrugged. "I don't know, but I've been seeing them around town. Kinda cool, huh?" She laid a stack of mail on Audra's desk and returned to the outer office.

It was nice to think that not everyone saw her father as a criminal, but was this just another way of portraying him as someone outside the law?

"Knock, knock."

She turned, and her mood lifted at the sight of Hud. He looked rumpled and windblown, but all the more handsome for it. But when he didn't return her smile, some of her happiness abated. "What's wrong?" she asked.

He stepped into her office and pulled the door closed behind him. "We found Roy Holliday," he said. "Or rather, we found his body."

"He's dead?" How could that be?

Hud took her arm and led her to the chair behind her desk, then handed her the water bottle from the corner of the desk. She drank, then pulled herself together. "That's a shock," she said. "Can you tell me what happened?"

"The coroner thinks he died six days ago."

She did the math. "But that would have been Wednesday. The day he was at my house."

"Yes. That's one reason I'm here. You may have been the last person to see him alive."

That sounded ominous. She took a deep breath. "Maybe go back a little and tell me everything. Where was he found? And when?"

"He was found at an illegal dump site a couple miles off Highway 50, in the Curecanti National Recreation Area. Someone—we don't know who— dumped a couple hundred yards of construction debris there a few weeks back. The Forest Service hired a contractor to haul everything away, and they found Holliday's body underneath a pile of broken drywall."

She made a face. "How horrible. If he's been out there five days—" Even in June, daytime temperatures could climb into the nineties, and there was so much wildlife out there…

"He hadn't been there five days," Hud said. "He may have been there only a few hours."

"Where was he before that?"

"We don't know for sure, but the coroner thinks he might have been kept in cold storage."

"In a refrigerator?" She couldn't even wrap her mind around the idea.

"Or a morgue or somewhere similar."

She shuddered. "That's bizarre. How did he die?"

"He was shot in the head. Small-caliber bullet. I need you to go over again everything he did and said when you saw him last Wednesday."

"Right." She rested her hands on her knees and thought a moment, then said, "When I opened the door to him, I don't remember another car parked on the street or in my driveway. I wasn't looking for one. But I think I would have noticed if one had been there. My house isn't set that far off the street and though it was early, it was quite light."

"What was his manner?" Hud asked. "How did he seem?"

"He was very relaxed. He apologized for coming to the house so early, but he really needed to talk to me. I asked if this was about a new enrollment and he asked again to come in and talk." She flushed, remembering how naive and vulnerable she had been. "He introduced himself as Roy Holliday, and I thought the name sounded familiar, but I thought I must have seen it on an application for enrollment. We've been getting a lot of those, now that word has gone out that we're moving to the new elementary school and doubling our capacity."

"When did you realize he was a reporter?" Hud asked.

"He said he was working on a story about Dad. He wanted to know if Dad helped me to get the contract for the new center, since TDC was building the facility. He asked me what it was like growing up with

Dane as a father, and if I had any idea what he was planning when he disappeared. I felt really foolish for letting him in."

"Did he act aggressive at all?"

"Not really. He took my phone away when I tried to call 911, but he just laid it on the back of the sofa. He was really very relaxed. Confident. When I told him I was leaving, he didn't try to follow me. He probably thought it would be a good opportunity for him to snoop around."

"Did you hear him leave?"

"No, but I was on the phone with you. When I got back into the kitchen and he was gone, I was surprised, but I guess he heard me on the phone and didn't want trouble."

"Did you think it was odd that the back door was standing open?"

"Not really. I figured he was in a hurry, and sometimes the latch doesn't catch all the way. You have to pull it hard until it clicks into place." She pictured that back door again and gasped. "Do you think someone *took* him from the kitchen?" she asked. "They forced him to leave and then killed him?"

"We're going to interview all the neighbors around the house and on the adjacent streets," Hud said. "Maybe one of them saw something."

"I can't believe all this is happening," she said. "It was bad enough when Dad pulled his disappearing act, but lately, every time I turn around, something horrible is happening." She put her head in her hands. "I'm ready for it to stop."

Hud rested his hand on her back. "What else has happened?" he asked.

She straightened. "Oh, it's more of a nuisance than anything. At least, I hope that's all it is."

"What?" He pulled the visitor's chair around beside her and sat.

"Oh, yesterday I got a call from the school superintendent, summoning me to his office. My day care and preschool are a private concern, not part of the school district, but the new elementary school is district property. TDC donated the land for the new school and gave them a big break on the construction costs. Rather than operate their own day care and preschool, the district decided to award a contract to a private concern. I'll actually be leasing my classroom space from the school district."

"What did the superintendent want to see you about?"

"He—Vernon Wells—was upset about what he termed all the negative publicity about me. I got him to admit the publicity was about my father, not me, and that I had nothing to do with it. But he said it looked bad to have the Trask name associated with this project."

"You have a contract, don't you?" Hud said. "There would be consequences for pulling out."

"Yes, and believe me, I'll fight him all the way if he tries to back out on the deal. But he said the contract has a morals clause and he could exercise that."

"On what grounds?"

"I don't know." She chewed at her lower lip, gut

churning. "But he might find a reason." She clasped her hands tightly together, wishing she could as easily contain the anxiety within her. "Have the police had any luck identifying 'Lawrence'?"

Hud shook his head. "I haven't heard anything. Any word from your lawyer?"

"No. She's filed some motions, and we're waiting on the judge."

He slipped his arm around her. "What you need is a night out. You still owe me a dinner out."

"I do, don't I?"

"A movie and Thai food?"

"I want to see something funny. I need a good laugh."

"I think we can manage that."

THEY SAW A comic mystery that was both silly and fun. Sitting next to her in the dark theater, laughing at outrageous situations, Hud felt transported to another world, one where pain and trouble couldn't intrude, where he and Audra could be more than a cop and a crime victim, but friends.

Over pad thai and pineapple fried rice, Audra told him about the Free Dane Trask sticker someone had left on her desk. "It's probably one of the teachers," she said. "Depending on who it is, they're either trying to cheer me up or giving me a hard time."

"I've seen those around," Hud said. "Apparently your dad has fans."

"I don't get it," she said. "The media have made him out to be so horrible."

"Some people like to root for the underdog. And he has a lot of friends in the community—veterans he helped through the veterans' group he founded."

"Welcome Home Warriors was very dear to his heart. He helped so many men and women to find jobs or get counseling, or simply to find friends with others who shared common experiences." She rested her chin in her hand, a wistful expression on her face. "Those people were really his tribe. I was more shocked that he left them behind than that he left me."

The words tugged at his heart, and he searched for something he could say to comfort her. But Audra wasn't looking for sympathy. She squared her shoulders. "Enough of that. I'm not going to get all maudlin, I promise. Tell me about your family."

So he told her about growing up with a younger brother and sister, a father who worked in marketing and a mother who ran a women's boutique. "They don't understand why I wanted to be a cop, but they never tried to talk me out of it. My other brother works in marketing like my dad, and my sister works for a big corporation in sales. When we get together at the holidays, the four of them have a lot more to talk about than I do." He shrugged. "It's okay. I like my life, even if it's not the one they wanted for me."

"My dad never put any expectations on me," she said. "I think my mother would have liked if I had married money, or done something more glamorous than teach toddlers how to tie their shoes, but she's too involved in her own dramas to worry much about mine. My dad always said he just wanted me to be happy."

"I like him better, the more you tell me about him."

"I think he'd like you, too," she said.

If they ever met, it might be with Hud pointing a gun at Trask and ordering him to accompany him back to the station. He probably wouldn't like Hud much then, but there was always hope they could get past that.

He took Audra home and kissed her good-night at the door, a lingering kiss full of passion and promise. He wanted to stay with her, but he wouldn't press. When she was ready, she'd let him know.

He had just turned onto the highway leading out of town when his phone signaled an incoming text message. He pressed the button to have his car's system read the text out loud.

"From Audra," the mechanical voice intoned. "Come back. Spend the night."

He did a U-turn in the middle of the highway. "Text Audra I'm on my way," he ordered.

She met him at the door, dressed in the same silky robe that had so distracted him when he arrived the evening when the private detective had trespassed. "What took you so long?" she said, pulling him inside and shutting the door behind him. Then she slipped her arms around him and kissed him, a kiss that pulled him under, out of the real world of unsolved crimes and petty annoyances into a universe where the two of them were the only things that mattered.

He broke the kiss and pushed back the edge of the

robe, the sight of her nude body stirring him more than all his fantasies. He pulled her to him, smoothing his hands down her sides, then bringing them up to cup her breasts. He looked into her eyes, watching her pupils widen and darken as he brushed his thumbs across her nipples, a deep pull in his groin as the tips hardened and pressed into his palm.

"Oh, yes," she whispered, arching to him. He bent to take the tip of one breast in his mouth, swirling his tongue around the areola, the tension inside him building as she gasped. She smelled of peaches and vanilla and tasted slightly sweet. She clutched at his head, fingers digging into his scalp, the softness of her breast against his cheek. He closed his eyes, determined to savor the moment, determined not to lose it in a rush of need and heat.

He slipped his hand between her thighs, her skin warm and softer than any satin. He entered her with one finger, then two, feeling her tighten around him. She rocked forward, pressed against him, making incoherent sounds of pleasure as he dropped to his knees and sealed his mouth over her center, tasting sweet and sour and female.

He teased with his tongue, fingers still stroking inside her. She moaned, the sound resonating through him, his erection pulsing in response. He experimented with different rhythms and pressures until she rocked against him, impatient. Demanding.

He smiled against her, delighting in her pleasure, delight building and expanding as she came, thrusting hard against him, spasming against his fingers.

She sagged against him, and he stood, gathering her close once more and leading her to the bedroom.

They lay down together and she opened her eyes and looked up at him, eyes still dark with desire. "Oh, that was very good," she said. "But you and I are just getting started."

Chapter Eight

Audra had lit candles in anticipation of Hud's arrival, and now she watched him undress in the golden light, revealing a lean, muscled body, strong legs and arms, and an erection that made her tighten in anticipation, desire building once more. He slid under the sheets beside her and reached for her, and she rolled on top of him, reveling in the feel of him along her full length.

Then she broke the kiss and straddled him, smoothing her palms along his shoulders and down his chest, his erection hot and eager at the junction of her thighs. He reached up to cup her breasts, gently pinching her nipples until she gasped with pleasure. "Do you like that?" he asked.

"Oh, yes." She wrapped both hands around the length of his erection, stroking until his eyes lost focus, then leaned across to take a condom from the bedside drawer, unwrap it and roll it on.

He grasped her hips and guided her as she slid over him, and he arched up to drive deeper, beginning a rhythm that she quickly modified, a thrust and parry that satisfied them both. When he reached one hand down to fondle her, she silently thanked whoever had taught him that move and abandoned herself to pleasure.

She didn't know how long they rode that wave of pleasure, but when she climaxed for the second time that night she would have said she had never enjoyed anything more.

They fell asleep in each other's arms. When she woke again, sunlight was just streaming through the gap in her bedroom curtains, and the shower was running. She smiled and wrapped her arms around her herself. She loved that Hud was so passionate and intense, but he was also so much fun. She loved his bad jokes and flippant remarks, his silly faces and even his off-key singing in the shower.

She might even be falling in love with the man himself, but she pulled back from examining those feelings too closely. They had plenty of time to explore and see what developed. No sense rushing and maybe ruining everything.

HUD DIDN'T KNOW if he had the strength to leave a naked Audra in a warm bed, but by the time he was out of the shower, she was up and dressed and had coffee going. "The day starts early at a day care center," she told him after she kissed him good morning. She handed him a mug of coffee. "What time do you have to be at work?"

"Early, too." He sipped the coffee and welcomed the bitter jolt. "I'm going to try to interview Roy Holliday's live-in girlfriend today, to see if I can figure out what he was doing that got him in trouble with the wrong people."

"I don't envy you your job," she said.

"And I don't envy you yours." He shuddered. "I'd rather face down armed criminals than a room full of two-year-olds."

She laughed. "There are days when I would, too, come to think of it."

Hud might have taken the two-year-olds over the grieving woman he faced two hours later. Renee Delaware was pale and shaken, silent tears streaming down her face despite her efforts not to weep. "I'm sorry I'm such a mess," she kept apologizing. "I just can't believe he's gone. We were talking about getting married in the fall, and now that's never going to happen." She bit her lip, her face crumpling again.

Hud waited while she pulled herself together. "I'm sorry to have to bother you at a time like this," he said. "But I'm trying to get a picture of what he was working on, what enemies he might have."

"Anything to help find the person who did this." She blotted her eyes with a tissue and sniffed. "Ask me anything."

"What was Roy working on in the weeks before he died?" Hud asked.

"He was writing about Dane Trask. Anything he could find about the man. He was fascinated by him, and the news outlets were hungry for more stories, so Roy was giving them everything he could. He talked to people Dane worked with and veterans at Welcome

Home Warriors, people who said they'd seen him at Black Canyon—anybody who could give him a new angle on the story."

"Was there anything in particular he was excited about?"

She nodded. "When he left here Wednesday morning, he said he had a hot tip that could blow the case wide open."

Hud sat forward on the edge of the sofa. "Did he say what the tip was?"

"No. He just said it was big, and that he was going to talk to Dane's daughter, to see if she had more information."

"What did he work on?" Hud asked. "Did he have a laptop, or a desktop here at the house?"

"He had a laptop," she said. "He carried it with him almost everywhere. He had it with him when he left the house the morning…" She swallowed hard. "The last time I saw him. The officer who came here to tell me they'd found…they'd found his body…said they didn't find the laptop. And I guess they're still looking for his car."

Hud nodded. "Maybe the laptop will be in the car when we find it." Though he wasn't holding out much hope of that. "So he didn't have a computer here at the house where he might have kept some of the files?"

"No."

"What about backup?" he asked. "Did he use a flash drive, or back up to the cloud?"

"The cloud. I think he had some kind of program that automatically backed up everything."

"Do you remember the name of the program?"

She shook her head. "I'm sorry, I don't."

There weren't that many. Hud had copies of the more common ones on his unit at Ranger headquarters. "Do you know his log-in information?" he asked. "His username and password? Maybe something he used for most things?" Most people didn't bother having very many different log-ins and passwords.

"I'm sorry, I don't."

"Was there somewhere he would have written them down?"

"I don't know." Her eyes filled with tears again. "I really want to help you, but I don't know. His work was his work, you know?"

"No, you're doing fine," Hud said. "Did he keep a diary or an appointment book or anything like that?"

"It was all on his phone," she said. "The officer said they haven't found that, either."

"We'll get records of his calls from his carrier," Hud said. "Do you know which one he used?"

"Yes. We both have Verizon."

That would make things a little easier. "The call record will help us figure out who he was working with." And maybe who he had talked to before he was killed. It might even be his killer.

"The officers who came here searched his desk." She nodded toward an old oak desk in the corner of the living room. "They took a few things, but there wasn't much here. And I found a few more things I saved for you."

She stood and collected a box from the kitchen

table and handed it to him. "It's copies of a lot of the articles he wrote about Dane Trask, and a few other things he wrote recently. And I wrote out what I remembered about what he had been doing in the days before he disappeared."

"That's great," Hud said. "That will be really helpful." Later, Hud would read through these and build a database that could help him figure out who might have wanted the reporter out of the way. He stood, the box tucked under one arm. "If you think of anything, call me, anytime." He handed her one of his cards. "Especially if you think of that log-in information. Even if you're not sure it's for his backup files, it might be useful to us."

"I will," she promised, and walked him to the door.

She stood in the doorway and watched as he walked to his cruiser, a slight, sad figure, alone as only the grieving can be. He felt sorry for her, but told himself the best thing he could do was find the person or persons who had killed her fiancé.

Instead of going back to Ranger headquarters after his visit with Renee, he stopped by Canyon Critters Daycare. He spotted Audra on the playground, surrounded by a group of toddlers, and walked over to join her. The children stared, wide-eyed, at his uniform and weapon and, aware of their audience, Hud didn't kiss Audra, though he wanted to.

"Is something wrong?" she asked, anxiety in her eyes.

He supposed he couldn't blame her, since the only other times he'd stopped by her workplace had been to deliver bad news. "Nothing's wrong," he said. "I was in the neighborhood and thought I'd say hello."

"That's nice." The warmth of her smile took away the sting of her earlier wariness. She turned to the toddlers still gathered around her. "Everyone go play while I talk to Officer Hudson."

The children moved away in groups of two or three, some toward a play structure with swings and a miniature climbing wall, others to where two teachers were organizing a game with plastic balls and bats. "It was such a beautiful day I couldn't stand sitting in my office another minute," Audra said.

"It is," he agreed. "I may have to find an excuse to hike out into the park this afternoon."

"That shouldn't be—" But a wail from the play structure stopped her in mid-sentence. They both turned to see a thin child with long white-blond hair sitting in the dirt, bawling.

"Get up, you big baby." Another little girl, with long brown hair and rosy cheeks, stood over the first child.

"You pushed me!" the first girl sobbed.

"I did not. You're just clumsy. Ugly and clumsy." The dark-haired girl scuffed her shoe in the dirt, the resulting dust settling on the crying child.

Audra rushed to the girls, arriving at the same time as an older woman with short, graying hair. "April, get up," the older woman ordered. "You're not hurt."

"How do you know she's not hurt?" Audra squatted beside April. "Honey, are you hurt?"

"I scraped my elbow." The child displayed a bleeding elbow.

"Come on, then, let's get you into the office and clean you up." Audra took the child's arm and helped her up.

"I'll see to it." The older woman took hold of April. "You get back to your visitor." She sent Hud a narrow-eyed glance.

"April, go with Mrs. Keplar," Audra said.

Mrs. Keplar pulled April toward the building. Audra turned to the other little girl. "I didn't push her," the child said before Audra could speak. "I was trying to do like you said and be her friend and play with her, and she's so clumsy she can't even do that right."

"Mia." Audra spoke quietly. "Calling April clumsy and a crybaby is not being her friend."

"But she is clumsy and she is a crybaby." Mia's face was flushed. She looked at the children who had gathered around. "I don't want to be friends with her and you can't make me." She stalked away, half a dozen others following her.

Hud walked over to stand by Audra. "Little April looks like she'll be okay," he said. "No broken bones."

"I'm afraid there's more to this than a fall off the play structure," she said. "Mia—the girl who just left—has been bullying April. April is very shy and timid and I'm afraid that's made her a target for Mia." She turned to him, her face a mask of anguish. "I don't understand why anyone would want to bully someone else. And Mia and April are both so young.

What is this kind of behavior going to do to both of them?"

Her distress pinched at him, and he struggled for something to say to ease her frustration, but as much as he was used to being in charge and having all the answers, he had none now. "I'm sorry you're having to deal with this," was all he could manage. "I can see how much it upsets you."

"Of course it upsets me. It should upset anyone." She touched his shoulder. "I really need to go in and check on April."

"No problem." He took a step back. "I'll talk to you later."

He returned to his cruiser, a dull ache in the middle of his chest. Of course Audra disliked bullies. Anyone would.

Would she dislike him if she knew he had been a bully? He thought he had put all that behind him a long time ago, but maybe there were some mistakes you could never entirely live down.

AFTER AUDRA LEFT the playground, she found April with Jana in the four-year-olds' classroom. "Hold still. I know it stings, but I need to clean it up. And will you please stop crying?" Audra heard Jana's scolding before she reached the room.

Both April and Jana looked up when Audra entered. "I've got this under control," Jana said, tossing aside a cotton ball and reaching for a bandage.

"It sounds to me like you're losing your temper," Audra said, her own voice calm. "Finish up here and

I'll stay with April while you see to the other children."

"I don't need—"

"And I need you to see to the rest of your class while I stay with April." Audra put more steel in her voice. Jana made a face, but stuck the bandage on April's elbow, then stood and stalked out of the room.

"How are you feeling, honey?" Audra asked. She began to put away the first aid supplies.

April sniffed. "Okay, I guess."

"What happened before you fell?"

More sniffling, then April said, "Mia asked me if I wanted to play on the swings. I said yes, and she offered to push me. But she pushed too hard and the swing went too high. I was scared. I told her not to do it and she just laughed and said we were playing and I had to play nice. I was really scared, so I tried to get off the swing and I fell. And she called me a crybaby."

Audra held back a sigh. Had Mia set up the situation to frighten April? Or did she simply not know how to play with a timid child? Audra was debating how best to approach this when Brenda rushed into the room. "You have a phone call you need to take," she said.

"Take a message," Audra said. "I have something else I need to see to."

"I really think you need to take this." Brenda glanced at April, then leaned closer. "It's April's mom," she whispered.

Audra frowned. "All right. You stay with April until Mrs. Keplar returns with the other children."

Audra shut the door to her office, took a deep breath, then answered the phone. "Hello, Mrs. Patrick," she said. "What can I do for you?"

"You can tell me why you continue to allow my daughter to be bullied. Why there wasn't proper supervision on the playground this afternoon. Why my daughter was put into a situation where she could have been badly hurt."

How had Mrs. Patrick already heard about this incident? Someone must have telephoned her, but who? Brenda? Jana? Now didn't seem the appropriate time to ask.

"I was on the playground this afternoon, Mrs. Patrick," she said. "April and Mia were playing on the swings and appeared to be having a good time—and then April was on the ground crying. I take it she jumped out of the swing because she was afraid."

"You shouldn't have let her anywhere near that little bully," Mrs. Patrick. "What if April had broken her arm? I can't believe this. I'm coming over there right now and I'm withdrawing April from your school. I want her ready to go, with all her things, and I expect a full refund of this month's fees."

Not waiting for an answer, Mrs. Patrick hung up. Audra dropped into her desk chair. She didn't blame Mrs. Patrick for being angry. Maybe Audra was even partly to blame, for encouraging Mia to befriend April. If she'd opted to separate the two girls instead of trying for reconciliation, maybe this never would have happened.

Resigned, she returned to the four-year-olds' classroom. April sat in a beanbag chair in the reading nook, curled in on herself, while the rest of the class gathered around Jana, who was laying out items for what Audra thought was a science experiment. Audra cleared her throat and Jana looked up. "I just need a moment of your time," Audra said, and returned to the hallway.

Jana joined her a moment later. "What is it?" she asked. "I just got the children settled. I decided it was better to leave April to herself than to try to do anything with her."

"April's mother is coming to pick her up soon," Audra said. "I need you to gather all her belongings and have them ready to go. Mrs. Patrick is withdrawing her from school."

"That's probably for the best," Jana said. "I don't think April has the social maturity for a school like this."

Audra didn't want to hear Jana's opinions on the matter. "Did you call Mrs. Patrick?" she asked.

"A parent should always be contacted immediately if their child is injured at school."

"Then I'm the one who should have contacted April's mother."

"I'm her teacher. I saw it as my responsibility." Her clipped tone and the stubborn set of her jaw made it clear she wouldn't change her mind about this.

"Gather April's things, and I'll take her to the office with me to wait for her mother."

Jana returned to the classroom, and Audra leaned against the wall beside the door to wait. She couldn't help feeling judgment behind everything Jana said to her. Was that because the judgment was really there, or because of Audra's own insecurities?

If her father was around, she would call him and ask his advice. He had always done a good job of bolstering her spirits and helping her see solutions to problems. If he had died, she'd be grieving his departure. Instead, she felt a confusing mixture of anger and loss. He had sent messages to other people since his disappearance—why hadn't he made it a point to contact her?

April emerged from the classroom a few minutes later, backpack on her shoulder and her arms laden with a box that appeared to contain school papers and supplies, a water bottle, a bunch of paper flowers and a box of tissues. Audra forced cheerfulness into her voice. "Your mom's coming to pick you up. You can wait in my office until she gets here."

"Am I in trouble?" April asked, freckles standing out against her pale skin.

Audra melted in sympathy for the child. She'd been so focused on her own troubles without thinking about how April must feel. "You're not in trouble," she said, one hand on the girl's shoulder. "Not at all. Your mom just thought you might need a break."

April nodded. "Yeah. I do."

Mrs. Patrick arrived fifteen minutes later, tension radiating from her slender body. "Are you okay?" she asked April, accepting the box of belongings from her.

"I'm okay now." April displayed her bandaged elbow. "Mrs. Keplar fixed me up."

"I should hope so." Mrs. Patrick glanced at Audra, then looked away again. "I'm very disappointed things have come to this," she said. "But I hope you understand why I can't allow April to remain here, where she doesn't feel safe."

"I'm very sorry, Mrs. Patrick," Audra began. "I—"

"After reading the papers this morning, I was already thinking that this school was not the place for my girl." Mrs. Patrick slipped the backpack from April's shoulders as she spoke. "But after this, I'm sure of it."

"What do you mean?" Audra asked. "What was in the papers?"

Still the woman didn't look at her, fussing with smoothing April's hair. "I'm not saying you had anything to do with the murder of that young man, but it doesn't look good, does it? Come on, April, we need to go." She took her daughter's hand, then at last returned her gaze to Audra. "I'll expect that refund."

Then she was gone, leaving Audra stunned. Were the papers saying that she had something to do with Roy Holliday's death? Or had someone else died? She thought of calling Hud and asking him if he knew what Mrs. Patrick was talking about, but told herself that was silly. She could figure this out easily enough on her own.

She gathered her purse and her keys. "I have to leave early today," she told Brenda as she passed through her assistant's office.

"Are you okay?" Brenda rose from the chair behind her desk, her expression filled with concern. "You don't look well."

"I'm sure it's nothing. I just… I just need to get home." She all but ran from the building to the safety of her car. On the way home, she stopped at a convenience store and bought a copy of each of the two papers for sale—the *Denver Post* and a local paper. She didn't look at them until she was home, her door locked and her shades drawn. Then she sat at the kitchen table, took a deep breath and opened the local paper first. She stared at the bold black letters of the headline:

Holliday May Be Trask's Latest Victim—Trask's Daughter Last to See Reporter Alive.

Chapter Nine

Hud read the article that filled the front page of the Montrose paper, anger growing as he read. The piece reported how freelance reporter Roy Holliday had been found on public lands just outside Black Canyon of Gunnison National Park, a single gunshot wound to the back of the head. Holliday had been reporting on the Dane Trask disappearance, and Trask's daughter, Audra Trask, had been the last person Holliday was known to have spoken to before he died.

The article went on to detail Trask's disappearance and repeat the worst rumors about him—that he was accused of embezzling money from his former employer, TDC Enterprises, that he had been the chief suspect in the murder of a female hiker and was suspected in several other attacks on hikers, as well as theft from campers in the park. The writer concluded by alluding to unidentified "authorities" who "are not ruling out a link between Holliday's visit with Audra Trask and his death."

When he finished reading, Hud sat back in his chair, fury growing. He wanted to punch somebody

for filling the public's heads full of lies and speculation. Searching for a target, he spotted Faith Martin
across the room. As the department's liaison with
both the press and the Montrose Sheriff's Department, Martin would be most familiar with the play-
ers in this fiasco. He stalked to her desk and tossed
the paper onto it. "How do reporters get away with
lies like this?" he asked. "And who are the 'authorities' he's quoting?"

Martin, a petite woman whose brown curls fought
to escape the bun at the nape of her neck, removed
her earbuds and looked up at him, then, registering
his anger, studied the paper before her. Frown lines
formed between her neatly shaped eyebrows. "The
official statement I issued from this department said
nothing about Dane Trask or Audra Trask."

"Then someone leaked the information about
Audra."

"It could have been someone from the Montrose
police," she said. "They responded to the call at her
house the day Holliday disappeared. Or maybe the
reporter saw the item on the police report and put two
and two together."

"It's all speculation and innuendo," Hud said.
"Dane Trask isn't a suspect, and Audra didn't have
anything to do with Holliday's death."

Martin shrugged. "It's the kind of thing that sells
papers."

"It's wrong."

Martin looked up at him, her brown eyes calm.

"It's upsetting, but there's nothing we can do about it. We have more important things to focus on."

Right. He returned to the desk but didn't sit, still trying to calm down. He wanted to call Audra, but she'd still be at school. She wouldn't appreciate the interruption, and clearly, when he talked to her earlier she hadn't known about the article. He'd call later and break the news gently, just so she'd be prepared tomorrow.

He read the article again. The story didn't say anything about Roy Holliday's body being kept in cold storage before it was dumped. That was a heavy point in Trask's favor. Not only had he had no motive to kill the reporter, it was doubtful he had access to anyplace to stash the body.

As Hud flipped through the rest of the paper, searching for any further mention of Trask or Audra, he began to calm down. Martin was right. The paper had been featuring the Dane Trask story at every opportunity for weeks now. Readers were obviously hungry for this local mystery.

On page six of the paper he focused on a small article near the bottom of the page. TDC Fined for Falsifying Reports.

> *The EPA has levied fines in the amount of $350,000 against TDC Enterprises in connection with the cleanup of the Mary Lee mine earlier this year. TDC, which was awarded the contract to mitigate heavy metals and other contaminants at the former gold and silver*

*mine in the Curecanti Wilderness outside of
Montrose, has been found guilty of falsifying
some of its reports showing lower-than-actual
levels of contaminants. Though TDC has since
corrected the reports, and the mine site has
been deemed satisfactorily mitigated, the EPA
issued a statement saying, "It's important that
mistakes like this not go unpunished. The public
is entitled to accurate data about the projects
its tax dollars are funding."*

*TDC vice president Mitchell Ruffino told re-
porters at a press conference Tuesday morning that the reports were falsified by former
employee Dane Trask, who is himself subject
to a massive manhunt in Black Canyon of Gunnison National Park since disappearing there
six weeks ago. "TDC and its employees take
pride in the work we have done to completely
clean up the contamination at the Mary Lee
mine," Ruffino said. "We're disappointed that
the EPA sought to blame us for the actions of
one clearly troubled man, but as good public
citizens, we will pay the fines and continue to
set the kind of environmental example we hope
other corporations will follow."*

Hud sat back, digesting this information. From the
very first, Dane Trask had tried to focus attention on
the work TDC was doing at the Mary Lee mine. The
day his truck was found at the bottom of Gunnison
Gorge in the national park, he had left a flash drive

for his former administrative assistant. Hud himself had analyzed the contents of that flash drive, which contained parts of environmental assessments from the Mary Lee—reports showing much higher levels of contaminants than TDC had reported.

Later, Trask had mailed a press release to his former girlfriend, asking her to give it to reporters she knew. The press release—which had never been published—alleged that TDC had falsified the reports about the mine. Samples Trask's former admin collected from the site seemed to back up this assertion, but only a short while later, TDC held a ceremony to announce the mine was "fully mitigated"—and that appeared to be the case. So who was lying? Or was everyone shading the truth?

"What are you scowling about?"

Hud looked up to see Jason Beck standing at the corner of his desk. He straightened. "What's up?" he asked, ignoring his friend's question.

Beck sat on the corner of the desk. "I've been reinterviewing construction people, trying to establish some kind of connection to that dump site or Roy Holliday, but getting nowhere. What about you?"

"I talked to Holliday's girlfriend this morning. She said he was working on something big to do with the Dane Trask story. He'd been talking to everyone who knew Dane, searching for new angles to report, since the local paper was hungry for more stories from him. The girlfriend said Holliday had a 'hot tip' he wanted to talk to Audra about."

"No idea what the tip was?" Beck asked.

"None."

"Then we need to talk to the people Holliday talked to," Beck said. "One of them must have given him this tip—and it may be what got him killed."

Hud blew out a breath. "You're right. And I did get some names from her. We can get others from the stories he filed."

"Let's divide the list," Beck said. "I'd like to solve a case for a change, instead of beating ourselves up chasing Dane Trask."

"Did you see the latest edition of the local paper?" Hud asked.

"No, why?"

Hud showed him the articles about Roy Holliday's murder and the EPA fine against TDC Enterprises. "It doesn't really help us, does it?" Beck said. "You don't think there's really a link between Audra and Holliday's death—other than he wanted to ask her about something that might be related to his killer."

"I don't think that, but the public might," Hud said. "I guess I worry about how this might affect her. She's having a hard enough time, with her dad constantly in the news."

"So—something going on between you two?" Beck asked.

Hud shrugged. "Something." He wasn't ready to define his feelings for Audra. Not yet. Better to keep things loose and see what developed. Maybe it was a cop-out. Or maybe it was good protective instincts.

His phone buzzed, and he pulled it out to answer. His heart sped up when he saw Audra's name on the screen. Beck waved and walked away, and Hud turned his back on the room and answered the call. "I was going to call you later," he said.

"Do you think you could come over to my house? Now." No missing the strain in her voice.

He headed for the door, digging out his keys as he walked. "What's wrong?" he asked.

"Nothing. I mean, I'm not in any danger or anything. There are just a bunch of reporters here and I'd feel better if I wasn't alone."

"I'm on my way."

AUDRA HAD TRIED to be polite with the reporters. That was her first mistake. There were three of them—two women and a man. They had identified themselves and who they worked for, knocking on her door only minutes after she finished reading the article about Roy Holliday's death. She immediately forgot everything they told her in the shock of seeing them there, as if they had been waiting out of sight to pounce when she was most vulnerable.

Perhaps they had. She tried to tell them she had no comment, but they continued to fire questions at her, the words as stinging as gravel thrown at her. Finally, on the verge of tears, she had retreated into the house, where she sat now, huddled in the darkness, feeling foolish and ashamed. She hated cowering in here, as if she truly had something to hide. Her father, she was sure, would not have put up with such behavior. But she wasn't as strong as Dane was. All she wanted was to go to sleep and to wake up tomorrow to find her life was back to normal, with her father home and plans for her new school moving forward.

Voices rose, and she moved to the front door and risked a peek outside. Hud was making his way up the walkway, shoving past the reporters—who had been joined by two more people now. They shouted questions at Hud, who moved past them, stone-faced.

She opened the door and stepped outside. As one, the group around Hud left him and surged toward her. "Why are the police here?" one of the women demanded. "Does this have anything to do with Roy Holliday's death?"

Hud reached her and took her arm. "Let's go back inside," he said, speaking softly but firmly.

She shrugged out of his grasp. "No," she said. "Maybe if I say something they'll leave."

"I don't think—"

But the reporters had moved in. "What was your relationship to Roy Holliday?" one asked.

"I didn't know Roy Holliday," she said. "He came to my house pretending to be the parent of one of my students and after I let him in he questioned me. I refused to talk to him and called the police. When the police arrived, he was gone. That's the whole story and that's all there is to it."

"Do you think your father killed him?" another reporter asked.

"No. Why would my father kill him?"

"To protect you from being harassed," someone said.

"That's ridiculous. My father didn't have anything

to do with Roy Holliday or his death. In fact, he hasn't done half the things you people insinuate he's done. For you to try to make him out as a murderer is disgraceful."

She probably could have said more, but Hud succeeded in pushing her inside and closing the door behind her. She pressed her back to the wall and closed her eyes, fighting tears, waiting for her heart to slow. When she opened her eyes again, Hud was watching her. "I imagine that will all be in the paper tomorrow, with some sensational headline," she said.

"Probably." He held out his arms. "Come here."

She sighed as he wrapped her in an embrace, and she rested her head on his shoulder. "I know I shouldn't have talked to them, but I couldn't listen to them say those things about my father. He doesn't have anyone else to defend him."

"It's okay," he said. "Maybe it helped to get some things off your chest."

"It did help, some." She pulled back far enough to look into his eyes. "Thanks for coming over. Part of me wishes I were strong enough to stand up to this myself, but the rest of me is really glad you're here."

"There's no weakness in relying on your friends," he said, but the tenderness in his eyes made her wonder if he was thinking of himself as more than a friend. Was she?

She pulled away and walked into the kitchen, where she poured a glass of water. He followed. "How did it go after I left the school this afternoon?" he asked. "With the little girls?"

"Not good." She took a long drink of water, then set the glass on the counter. "April's mother withdrew her from school. She's furious that this happened with a bunch of adults standing around, supposedly watching. I guess in her shoes I'd feel the same. But the worst of it was, as she was leaving, she said something about how, though she didn't believe the things the papers were saying about me, it didn't look good, did it? I rushed right out and bought a paper, then came home. I had just read the article in the *Daily Press* about Roy Holliday and my and my dad's supposed role in the murder when those reporters showed up."

"Did you see the other article in the paper?" he asked. "About TDC?"

She groaned. "There were others? What did they say?"

"The EPA is fining TDC for falsifying environmental reports about the Mary Lee mine—the very thing your father was accusing them of."

"That's something, I guess," she said. "I hope Dad sees it, whatever he's up to."

"Except TDC places the blame on him," Hud said. "They say he falsified the reports."

She shook her head. "He wouldn't. The thing people don't realize—can't realize unless they know him—is that my father doesn't lie. He just doesn't. And he'd have no reason to do so in this case." Agitation bubbled up again. "I can't stand people saying all these bad things about him and there's no way to defend him. It's not just what they say—it's how it feels.

Like I'm a little girl, being bullied all over again. The name-calling and lying—it feels the same."

"Words can hurt as much as blows," he said. "We don't always think about it, but they can."

"I hate bullies!"

She wanted him to pull her to him once more. Instead, he took a step back, mouth tight. A chill settled between them. "What is it?" she asked. "What's wrong?"

He shook his head. "Nothing. But if you think you'll be okay now, I have to go."

"Oh. Of course. But I don't understand. Did I say something to upset you?"

"It's okay." He smiled, but it wasn't convincing. "If you need anything later, just call."

Then he was gone, the door closing softly behind him. She followed and locked the door, listening to the reporters outside calling out questions, which he didn't answer. Something had happened just now to change the whole mood between them. She had said she hated bullies—but why would that upset him? Of course she didn't really hate a little girl like Mia— she hated the child's behavior. If Hud didn't like her word choice, why didn't he say so?

That moment when she had been in his arms had felt so warm and comforting. Now she felt more desolate and alone than before.

"WHAT AN IDIOT!" Hud cursed himself as he drove away from Audra's home. The look on her face when he'd left her made him feel like more of a jerk than

ever. He'd overreacted to her declaration that she
hated bullies—as if she had declared she hated him.
But what would she think if she knew he'd once been
the number one bully in his high school—a boy so
cruel and relentless he had driven a fellow classmate
to attempt suicide?

His stomach still knotted at the memory. He had
come a long way since his mixed-up childhood, but
would Audra believe that? Would her history as the
object of a bully's taunts allow her to see past how
truly awful he had once been?

He was still preoccupied with these thoughts when
he returned to Ranger headquarters. "There's someone here to see you," Officer Reynolds said as he
walked in. He nodded toward Hud's desk, where
Renee Delaware sat, focused on the phone in her
hand.

"Ms. Delaware, how can I help you?" he asked,
approaching her.

She looked up and slid the phone into the back
pocket of her jeans, then dug a piece of paper from the
front pocket. "I found this when I was going through
the drawer of the nightstand on Roy's side of the bed,"
she said. "I think it might be his log-in username and
password."

Hud studied the series and numbers and letters
scribbled in blue felt-tip pen on the paper. H0liday95
and 164951225. "What makes you think this is his
log-in and password?" he asked.

"His birthday is…was… April 16 and he was born
in 1995. Christmas is 12-25—his favorite holiday and

a play on his last name." She pressed her lips together, clearly reining in her emotions.

Hud nodded. "Thanks," he said. "And thank you for stopping by. This could be a big help."

"Nothing can bring him back," she said. "But I think it really would help if you could find out who killed him. I know people didn't always like him asking questions, but that was his job, and he was good at it. He didn't deserve to die because of it."

"We'll let you know if we find anything," Hud said. "Thank you again for coming in."

She nodded, then stood and left.

Hud settled behind his desk and pulled up an automatic data backup program he knew to be common with journalists. He was entering Roy Holliday's log-in information when Reynolds approached his desk. "You're working on the Holliday murder, right?" he asked.

Hud nodded, still focused on the computer.

"Delta County Sheriff's Department found his car this morning," Reynolds said. "Abandoned behind some storage units out in Whitewater."

"Oh?" Hud looked up, alert. "Did they find anything in it? His computer?"

Reynolds shook his head. "I sent you a copy of the report, but the gist of it is the car was stripped, the interior gutted. They even removed the seats, then set fire to what was left."

"Whitewater is a long way from where Holliday's body was found," Hud said.

"Less than an hour's drive," Reynolds said. "There

aren't any neighbors near the place, so they haven't been able to determine when the vehicle showed up there."

"That was Holliday's fiancée who was in here just now," Hud said. "She found a username and password that may get us into the cloud storage where Holliday backed up his computer files."

"Let's hope his killer didn't get there first," Reynolds said.

Hud nodded and went back to work. He typed in the password, pressed Enter and waited. A thrill shot through him as the screen filled with a file directory. "Did you get something?" Reynolds leaned in closer.

"Yeah." Hud began typing, sorting the files by date, most recent to oldest. "It looks like over a hundred files here. This could take a while."

"Then I'll leave you to it." Reynolds clapped him on the back.

Hud didn't hear him leave. He was already deep into the hunt for anything that might lead them to a killer.

Chapter Ten

Audra arrived at work the next morning, prepared to deal with Jana and Mia and the whole bullying situation. She'd decided to implement a school-wide anti-bullying curriculum, and had located some age-appropriate resources the teachers could use in the classroom. She would take the sad situation with April and turn it into a program everyone involved could be proud of—a model for other schools like hers to follow, even.

But she forgot all of this when a pale and anxious Brenda met her at the front door. "Have you seen the papers this morning?" Brenda asked. "Or watched the news?"

"No." Audra didn't like to start her day with strife and bad news, so she kept her television off and her radio tuned to her favorite music station on her drive in to work.

Brenda clutched her wrist. "It's bad," she said. "I'm so sorry, but it is. I've already had calls from two parents, saying they're going to withdraw their children from school. I put the phone back to the answering service after the first two. I didn't know what else to do."

"What's going on? Why do they want to withdraw their children?" Audra's hands shook as she opened the door to her office.

"I left a copy of the paper on your desk." Brenda bit her lip. "I don't even know if what it says is true, but people believe it's true, and I guess that's just as bad." Then she turned and hurried from the room, as if determined to outrun a storm.

Audra shut the door behind her and stared at the paper on the desk blotter. Even upside-down, she could read the headline: Dane Trask's Daughter Defends Father, Despite Their Troubled Past.

She frowned. She and her father didn't have a troubled past. They'd always gotten along well. He had always been a part of her life, and he had always been the one person in the world she could count on. With growing dread, she moved around the desk and sank into the chair. Then, as if she were approaching a poisonous snake, she cautiously leaned forward and began to read.

The beginning of the story wasn't bad—a rehash of yesterday's encounter with the press outside her house, and a somewhat garbled quote in which she said people calling her father a murderer was disgraceful. But the second paragraph sent a stabbing pain through her. "To some, Audra Trask's defense of her father might come as a surprise, considering that in her late teens, her father had her forcibly committed in an attempt to deal with her out-of-control drug addiction. Since then, others close to Trask say Audra has drifted in and out of his life, Trask always stepping forward to bail her out of trouble when needed. Most recently, Trask may have played a role in his daughter being awarded the contract for a new preschool and day care facility on the campus of a new elementary school TDC Enterprises is constructing in the northeast part of the county. At the time of Trask's disappearance, his daughter admitted she hadn't spoken to her father for two weeks."

She struggled to breathe, to overcome the red mist of rage that clouded her vision. The paper made her sound like a junkie whose father had had to send her away in a straitjacket—a spoiled daughter who only turned to Dad when she needed money or help out of trouble. Yes, she had become addicted to prescription painkillers in her late teens and yes, her father had persuaded her to go to rehab, and had paid for the treatment, or at least the portion not covered by his health insurance policy. But there had been no force involved. Audra had been desperate for help, and so grateful her father had come to her rescue at a time when she felt so powerless.

As for the rest, it was all lies. She had not been "in and out" of her father's life. She hadn't spoken to him in the two weeks before he disappeared because she had been visiting friends in France. And he had nothing to do with her getting the contract with the school district—Dane was an engineer with TDC, not someone with any kind of influence over the local school board.

Steeling herself for more bad news, she continued reading the article. After a summary of Dane's disappearance and the various accusations against him, her gaze landed on a quote attributed to Jana Keplar. "Since taking a position as a teacher at Canyon Critters Daycare, it's become clear to me that Ms. Trask has some problems she needs to address. I think the school district will be reassessing whether she is really the person they want operating their new day care and preschool."

Audra made a strangled sound in her throat, then sucked in a deep breath. *Think*, she reminded herself. What was she going to do about this? There were so many things wrong with this article. She needed to address them all. There was Jana, of course. Should she fire the woman for speaking against her? No—she wanted to fire her, but that would only cause problems, not the least of which is she didn't have anyone to take over Jana's class. And the students and parents clearly loved her. If Audra fired Jana, she'd come off looking vindictive and immature. Not the sort of person anyone would want to trust. So she'd leave Jana be for now.

What else? She probably needed to contact the school superintendent and persuade him that she was capable, stable and exactly the person he wanted for the new facility. But how could she do that when he was already upset about her father? This article wasn't going to help her standing in his eyes. She needed to find someone who had more influence than she did to speak up on her behalf. She'd have to think about that one.

She scanned the article once more. Who were these mysterious "others close to Trask" who had said she was "in and out of his life"? Not his former girl-friend, Eve Shea. She and Audra had always gotten along great. She didn't know of any other women her father had dated recently. Was it someone from Welcome Home Warriors? The men and women who were part of the veterans' group Dane had founded didn't really know her. But she had attended events there when her dad invited her, so they would have seen her with him and realized how close they were.

Coworkers? A sensation went through her as if a nerve had been touched. Ever since her father had disappeared, TDC Enterprises had done everything they could to discredit him. Was this simply one more way to get back at her father, by lying about his re-lationship with her?

She folded the newspaper and tucked it away. In the background, the phone rang, falling silent after three rings as the answering service picked up. She'd have to deal with those calls from disgruntled par-ents soon, mustering every bit of confidence possible to persuade them that the article was filled with lies and exaggerations, and their children were in good hands with her.

Her father had taught her to stand up for herself. When people went after you, you didn't sit back and take it—you fought back. But how was she going to fight back against this onslaught, when she wasn't even sure who her enemy was?

HUD FELT SICK to his stomach as he listened to two newscasters discuss Audra Trask's "sad history" of drug addiction and her stormy relationship with her father. "An old familiar story," the male newscaster said. "One many parents have dealt with."

"But one that has captured the public's interest, now that Dane Trask is the most wanted man in the county, if not the state," his female counterpart concluded.

Hud switched off the television and sank back in his chair. Audra had been an addict? It shouldn't surprise him. Drug addiction cut across all socioeconomic levels. As a DEA agent, he dealt with the ugly side of addiction—people who stole from their parents, who prostituted themselves and broke ties with everyone who loved them, at the mercy of their addiction. Good for her getting past that—so many people didn't. And he was pretty certain he'd know now if she was hiding any current addiction. The woman didn't even drink!

As for her relationship with Dane, she had always spoken of her father warmly. If they had had their difficulties in the past—and what parent and child hadn't?—she didn't consider them significant enough to share with him. That part of the news story had been more speculation than fact, the word "allegedly" liberally sprinkled in the reporting.

He tried to call Audra's cell, but his call went

straight to voice mail. She was probably getting calls from the press and most of the people she knew. Fine. He'd go to her. He was supposed to continue working his way through Roy Holliday's computer files, but so far that had turned up nothing. Whatever was in there to be discovered would have to wait a little longer. Things had been awkward between him and Audra when he'd left yesterday—all his fault. He'd find a way to make it up to her now. She didn't need to be facing this alone.

Everything at the school looked normal to him— no crowds of reporters or irate parents. The playground was empty, but kids didn't have recess all day, did they? But inside, things were definitely more tense. The phone rang and rang, and when Hud entered the office, Audra's assistant scarcely looked up from her computer. "Audra isn't here right now. You'll have to come back later," she said, in the tone of voice of someone who had repeated the same phrase over and over all morning.

"I'm Officer Mark Hudson," he said in his sternest voice.

The woman's head snapped up. She stared at him, wide-eyed. "Is something wrong?" she asked. "Is Audra in more trouble?"

"She's not in trouble," he said. "Where is she?"

"Can I help you with something, Officer?" A tall woman with gray streaks in her short dark hair stepped out of Audra's office. She looked familiar, but Hud couldn't remember her name.

"Who are you?" he asked.

"I'm Jana Keplar." She moved toward him. "I'm helping Brenda since Audra isn't in."

"Where is Audra?" he asked, annoyance giving a harder edge to his voice.

Jana's expression, which he would have labeled smug, didn't change. "I think she went home. With a headache."

The constant ringing of the phone was enough to give anyone a headache. But things must have been very bad for Audra to leave the school. She didn't strike him as one who would abandon her post. "I'm surprised she left," he said.

"Oh, she didn't want to go." The assistant spoke from behind him. "Jana and I had to talk her into it. With the news reports and everything, it's been a little wild here. No one can get anything done. We decided if she wasn't here, there would be no one for the parents and reporters to talk to, so they'd give up and leave us alone." She looked toward the phone, which, after a brief respite, had started up again.

"Is that working?" Hud asked.

"It worked with the people who came in person," Brenda said. "We're letting the calls go to voice mail."

"We'll be lucky if we don't have to close the school after this," Jana said. "But maybe it would be for the best, in the long run."

Hud didn't wait to hear more. He left and drove to Audra's house. The relief that washed over him when he spotted her car in the driveway surprised him. He hadn't been able to admit to himself that he was half-afraid she might do something drastic, such as confronting reporters, or worse, that she might try to harm herself.

He had to ring the bell twice before she answered. She looked pale and a little drawn, but if she had cried about this, she had done so earlier. "I didn't answer right away because I thought you might be a reporter," she said, leading the way into the living room.

"I heard the news reports," he said. "How are you doing?"

"I've been better."

"You should have called me right away. You shouldn't have to deal with this alone."

She shrugged. "I thought maybe you wouldn't want to see me again."

The words hurt, but he couldn't say he didn't deserve them. "I know I was a jerk last time we spoke," he said. "I'm sorry."

She faced him at last. "You're sorry? I'm the one who should be apologizing, for not being honest with you about my past. I did struggle with drug addiction—but it was nothing like the papers made it out to be. And everything they said about my relationship with my father was a lie." She dropped onto the sofa, elbows on her knees, face in her hands.

Hud sat beside her, close, but not touching. "Your past is your past," he said. "Where you've been tells me a lot about you, but it's not as important as where you are now—who you are now."

She sat up straighter but didn't look at him. "What does my past tell you about me? That I was a low-life addict? Someone with no self-control who used drugs as an escape?"

The harshness in her voice was like a barb under his skin. "It tells me you had real pain in your life," he said. "Pain you tried to overcome, maybe the only way you knew how. But you got past that. You found the strength to overcome an addiction that a lot of people struggle with. I think that probably made you wiser and more empathetic than a lot of people."

The tears came then, sliding down her cheeks, though she didn't make a sound. He took her hand in his, and she leaned over until her head rested on his shoulder. He fished a handkerchief from his pocket, and she took it. Neither of them said anything, but he felt some of the tension ease from her body. After a while, she began to talk. "I was nineteen. I tore my knee up skiing and had to have surgery. The doctor gave me Vicodin for the pain in my knee, but it made me feel better in other ways, too. I'd just broken up with my first serious boyfriend. My mom had married again, and that put some distance between us. But the pills made me feel like I could cope." She shrugged. "I guess that's how a lot of people get hooked. I thought I could handle it. It wasn't like I was out on the street trying to score heroin or something. But I wasn't handling it. I wasn't handling anything."

"But you got help," he said. "You overcame the addiction."

"Dad is the one who saved me. He knew a lot about addiction—he worked with a lot of veterans who struggled through the group he founded here—

Welcome Home Warriors? Anyway, he got me the professional help I needed and paid for rehab, but mostly, he just listened." She sat up and angled toward him. "You know how in AA, people have sponsors—someone they can call, night or day, when they're feeling tempted? Dad was that for me."

"That's why you don't drink alcohol, isn't it?" he asked.

She nodded. "In rehab I learned that people with drug addiction problems also have a greater likelihood of becoming alcohol-dependent. I don't want to take a chance." She dabbed at her eyes, then returned the damp handkerchief. "So now you know my dark secret."

He looked down at the handkerchief, a smudge of her pink lipstick on one corner. "You're not the only one with secrets, you know," he said.

She stared at him. "Don't tell me you did drugs, too."

"No. I think maybe what I did was worse."

It was her turn to take his hand, her fingers soft and cool, twining with his. "No judgments," she said.

"Yeah, well, the reason I left the way I did yesterday was because you said you hated bullies, and I was a bully."

Confusion clouded her eyes. "You? But you're one of the nicest, most patient—"

"I was a bully," he repeated. "In high school. There was a kid in one of my classes—one of those awkward kids who doesn't fit in. He tried to be friends with me, and I lashed out. And I didn't just do it once.

I made him a target. I teased him and humiliated him." He swallowed hard. Even after all this time, it was hard to talk about. To think he had had that kind of darkness in him. "I don't know why I did it. I think—I think I was afraid of being like him. Of being the weak kid no one else liked. So I lashed out. It made me feel stronger. Safer." He bowed his head and squeezed his eyes shut, telling himself he wasn't going to break down. Not after all this time.

Her fingers traced gentle circles across the back of his hand. "What happened to change you?" she asked, her voice just above a whisper.

"The boy—his name was Cameron—tried to kill himself. His father found him. He'd…he'd tried to hang himself."

"Oh, Hud." She leaned her head on his shoulder once more.

But the worst was out. He felt stronger now. "Cameron told his parents what was going on. They told the school. I was expelled, and my parents put me in counseling, and the counselor referred me to a program for bullies. There were a couple of cops who volunteered with the program, and they got me interested in police work. I was lucky, really."

"You changed. I can't tell you how hopeful that makes me." She sounded as if she meant it.

"I was thinking about that little girl at your school. Mia," he said.

Audra nodded. "She's not a bad child. I know that. And I tried talking to her parents, but they refused to see that there was any problem. Her teacher is convinced that the whole problem was with April. Now that she is no longer enrolled, there won't be a problem. But I'd like to do what I can to address situations like this from both sides. In fact, I spent half the night looking up resources and planning a curriculum that would address bullying for all ages. It was going to be a model program. And then the news about my past addiction came out. I had parents calling all morning, wanting to withdraw their children, or at least demanding to know if what they had read was true."

"Your assistant told me they sent you home as a stalling tactic," he said.

"You went by the school?"

"When you didn't answer your phone, I checked there first."

"How was it? I hated to leave Brenda to deal with things alone, but under the circumstances, my presence there was only fanning the flames. I'm hoping, given a few hours, some of the most heated emotions will cool, though I'll have to address the situation one way or another."

"The phone was ringing a lot, but there were no parents, and no reporters, at the school when I was there. But your assistant—Brenda—wasn't alone. Jana Keplar was in the office with her."

Audra straightened, color flooding back to her face. "Jana had no business being in the office. She has a class to see to. And after what she said about me to reporters, she's lucky to have a job."

"I only heard the story on the television news," he said. "What did the papers say?"

In answer, she got up, retrieved a folded newspaper from her bag and thrust it at him. He scanned through the article, then shook his head. "Where do they get all this about your relationship with your father being rocky?"

"I don't know," she said. "But I'm guessing TDC. Anyone he worked with could claim to be close to him, and ever since he left, they've been doing everything possible to discredit him. This is just one more way to embarrass him."

He tossed the paper aside. "I'm sorry you're having to go through this," he said. "What can I do to help?"

She sat beside him once more and wrapped her arms around him. "You're already doing it," she said. "Right now."

IT WAS WELL after noon before Hud made it to Ranger headquarters. He'd called in earlier, claiming he needed to see to a personal matter and would be in late. Thankfully, no one had questioned him too closely. Audra had assured him she was fine, and while he wanted to get back to her as soon as possible, he knew he'd be working late, going through the rest of Roy Holliday's computer files.

So far he'd read through numerous drafts of articles Holliday had written—many about Dane Trask, but also features on Black Canyon of Gunnison National Park, and one profile of TDC Enterprises that delved into the history of the company, its principal officers and its current projects, which included the elementary school where Audra was scheduled to re-locate her business.

Other files consisted of transcripts of interviews, though Holliday had a maddening habit of identifying the people he interviewed only by their initials. Sometimes Hud was able to figure out that MC in one interview was Michael Carter quoted in an article Holliday had written, but other times the identities of the interviewees remained a mystery.

A third set of files seemed to consist of to-do lists, which included everything from "change oil" to "meeting with RJ 2:15." Using these lists and the dates the files originated, Hud was able to construct a rough schedule of Holliday's activities in the weeks prior to his death. He focused on appointments, most of which were either for interviews or research for articles, or with editors with whom Holliday worked.

He found a note that said "see AT" dated the day before Holliday disappeared. Was this a reminder to himself to stop by Audra Trask's house to try to interview her? The day before that was a note to "call MR" but Hud had not been able to determine who MR might be, and had found no reference to anyone with those initials in the files, and no interview or other notes about such a person. He was still waiting on Holliday's phone records.

Hud sat back and studied the schedule he had made of Holliday's activities in the days before the reporter died. He believed Holliday had made some kind of contact with the person or persons who killed him during that time. He had met up with them again shortly after he left Audra's house Wednesday morning. He and his car had been taken, Holliday killed and his body put in cold storage, then dumped, and his car and everything in it destroyed and dumped. Why? The most obvious answer was that in the course of his reporting, Holliday had come across information his killer or killers didn't want made public.

Holliday had primarily been working on the Dane Trask disappearance at the time of his death. Had he learned something about Trask?

He groaned and tried to rub the kink out of his neck. Time to share what he'd learned with the rest of the team. Maybe other eyes would see what he hadn't. Even though Holliday was dead, there was always a sense of urgency in a murder case. Too often, the murderer would strike again. Hud wanted to stop him before that happened.

He was on his way to the commander's office when his cell phone rang. "Officer Hudson," he answered.

"Martin Burns from Montrose PD. You're working on the Dane Trask disappearance, aren't you?"

Hud remembered the MPD detective who had questioned Richard Salazar. "I am," he said. "What's up?"

"Someone broke into Trask's house this morning. I figured someone from the Ranger Brigade would want to take a look."

"I'll be right over." Dane Trask's home had sat empty for seven weeks. Had the vacant property been too tempting for thieves, or was someone after something in particular?

Chapter Eleven

"A neighbor saw someone over here and called it in." Detective Burns met Hud in front of Dane Trask's home. Hud had been to the modest but elegant cedar-sided home once before, to collect Trask's electronics and search for anything that might aid them in discovering his purpose in disappearing. The Ranger Brigade's searches hadn't turned up anything of value, and they had left the house much as they found it, orderly but lifeless.

This time, someone else had been searching for something, and had destroyed any sense of order. Furniture had been overturned, the cushions and undersides of chairs and sofas slashed open. Books from the bookcases lay twisted on the floor, and the pots from dead or dying houseplants had been emptied onto the carpet. Every drawer and cabinet had been emptied, every picture taken from the wall and cut from its frame. A forensics team dressed in white coveralls and booties moved through the mess, taking photographs, dusting for fingerprints and searching for evidence.

"Whoever did this left behind an expensive watch

and high-end electronics," Burns said as he and Hud followed a carefully marked path through the chaos. "Though it's impossible to tell if they took anything else."

"Is every room like this?" Hud asked. They were in the kitchen now, broken dishes and opened packages of pasta and coffee littering the floor.

"Every one," Burns said.

Hud shook his head. "Then I don't think whoever did this found what they were looking for."

"What were they looking for?" Burns asked.

"I don't know." Was it someone from TDC, trying to find something to further discredit Trask? Was it the mysterious "Lawrence" who had paid the private detective to dig up information about Audra? Or someone else entirely, someone the Rangers weren't yet aware of?

"Detective! We've got something here." One of the forensics team, a tall woman with a braid of blond hair, approached, a plastic bag in her gloved hand.

Burns studied the bag, then leaned over and sniffed. "Heroin?" he asked.

"I think so," the young woman said.

"We'll test it to be sure," Burns said, and the woman left the room with the bag.

"Have you found anything to indicate Trask was into drugs?" Burns asked Hud.

"No," Hud said. "And we searched this place, and his office at TDC, right after he disappeared. We didn't find anything."

"So whoever was trashing the place left it behind?" Burns scratched behind his ear. "That's not something you just casually drop—especially since they haven't left so much as a hair behind, at least that we've discovered to this point.

"Maybe it was a clumsy attempt to discredit Trask," Hud said.

"Clumsy, all right." He looked around the room, then back at Hud. "I can't figure this guy out. He had everything going for him—great job, respect in the community, a good relationship with his daughter. Yet he chucks it all to play hide-and-seek in the national park. You're pretty sure he's still there, right?"

Hud nodded. "Pretty sure." Dallas Wayne Braxton had been definite in his identification of the man he had encountered on the hiking trail, and it didn't seem likely Trask would have stuck it out living rough for so many weeks and suddenly decided to move on.

"If we get any more information here, I'll let you know," Burns said.

"Thanks. I'll pass on anything we uncover on our end." And now he'd have to tell Audra about this latest development. He didn't want her deciding to drop by her father's place and discovering this mess.

They headed toward the door, but Burns paused to look back at the chaos. "Whatever Trask is up to, he sure ticked off somebody," he said.

Hud needed to find Trask—or the person who was after him—before Audra ended up the chief casualty of the battle.

WHEN AUDRA RETURNED TO work after lunch, the phones had stopped ringing off the hook and, while a few students had been kept home by their parents, only one child had been officially withdrawn. Audra breathed a little easier, believing she had weathered the worst of the latest crisis. People had realized their children were well cared for and happy and getting a good education at her school, and that mattered more to them than something that had happened in the past. Now if she could persuade the school district to think the same way, everything would be back on track again.

But that still left the problem of what to do about Mia and bullying. Her conversation with Hud had made her want to dig deeper and try to help the girl before a minor problem became a serious one. So she sent Brenda to fetch the child from Jana's classroom.

Brenda returned a few moments later, Mia, looking frightened, at her side. "Am I in trouble?" Mia asked as soon as she saw Audra.

"No," Audra said firmly. She looked at Brenda, who was still standing by Mia, taking all of this in. "Thank you, Brenda. Mia and I will be fine now."

"Then why did you call me out of class?" Mia asked after Brenda had left and shut the door behind her. "Mrs. Keplar said I shouldn't have to go to the office if I'm not in trouble."

Jana Keplar needs to keep out of this, Audra thought, but she said, "I wanted a chance to talk to you about what happened with April. But I promise, you're not in trouble. I want to hear your side of the story."

Mia slid into the chair next to Audra, her feet not touching the floor. She sat very straight, her hands in her lap. She was a pretty child, with an alert expression and an easy manner. An easy child to like. "I tried to be friends with April, like you asked," Mia said. "But the other girls made fun of me for hanging out with a baby."

And of course it was tough for a little kid to stand up to that kind of criticism, Audra thought. Children could be cruel. Then again, adults could be, too. "Sometimes, doing the right thing is more important than being popular," she said gently.

Audra's interpretation of the look Mia sent her was "adults can be so dumb." Okay, time to try another approach. She searched her memory for everything she knew about Mia. "You have a little brother, don't you?" she asked.

Mia nodded.

"Why doesn't he come to day care, too?"

"Mama says he can't come until he's out of diapers."

"But we take infants," Audra said. Was Mia's mother unaware of this?

"I know. I told her that, but she said the extra charge for babies is too high, so she's going to stay home with him." She pouted, yet still managed to look adorable. "I don't see why I can't stay home, too, but she said no. So she gets to be with him all day, while I have to be here."

Audra caught a glimmer of understanding. "That must be really hard," she said.

Mia swung her legs and looked away.

"I guess sometimes it's hard for you to be happy here at school, then, when you wish you were home," Audra said.

Mia shrugged. "I like school. But I miss my mom, too."

Audra wanted to pull the little girl close and rock her in her arms, but she wasn't sure how Mia—or her mother—would view that. Instead, she patted Mia's shoulder. "Thank you for talking to me," she said. "Starting soon, we're going to have some lessons that talk about being kind to everyone and not calling names. I think you'll be able to help your classmates with those lessons."

Mia looked relieved. "So I'm really not in trouble?"

"Not at all." What Mia had done to April was wrong. But the adults in her life were at fault, too, for not doing more to help her, as well.

When she was alone again, Audra called Mia's mother. "Mrs. Ramsey, this is Audra Trask, from Canyon Critters Daycare."

"If you're calling about Mia, I don't want to hear it," Mrs. Ramsey said. "I won't have her being made a scapegoat for other people's bad behavior."

"I am calling about Mia, but not because she's done anything wrong," Audra said. "She's a very sweet, smart child."

"Oh." Audra could almost feel the woman on the other end of the line deflating. "Then why are you calling? Are you fundraising or something?"

"No. I had a conversation with Mia this afternoon I thought would interest you."

"What has she been telling you?"

"Mia loves you very much. And she loves her little brother."

"Well, of course. She's a very loving child. And we love her."

"I know you do. But I think she's feeling a little left out, with you staying home with the baby all day and her coming here."

"Day care for infants is more expensive, and I was able to work out an arrangement with my employer to work from home, so it makes sense for me to be here with the baby. But trying to work with two children underfoot, especially one as lively as Mia, would be impossible."

"I understand. And I'm not calling to persuade you to put your son in day care. Not until you're ready."

"Mia loves going to school. She has so many friends there, and she's learning a lot. She's already in the second-grade reader."

"She's a very bright child. But bright children can also be very sensitive. I know you're sending Mia to school, even though you could keep her home, because you see the benefits to her. But to her four-year-old mind, she just sees herself being sent away while the baby gets all your attention."

"Are you saying this behavior of hers, with that other little girl, April—was just acting out because she's upset about the baby?"

"It could be," Audra said.

"Then what do you suggest I do?"

This was the opening Audra had been waiting for. "You could try keeping Mia home a couple of days a week. Just as an experiment. We offer that option for parents with flexible schedules."

"That would certainly save us money. But do you really think it would help?"

"It might. I think after a few weeks, Mia might decide on her own she wants to come to school every day. But it will be her decision then, not something forced on her."

"She's only four. It's my job to make decisions for her."

"Of course. But I really do think this could help."

"Then I'm willing to try. And thank you. I may have spoken a little harshly before."

Audra smiled. "You love your daughter, so of course you were sensitive to criticism of her."

"Thank you for understanding."

Audra ended the call and hung up the phone. One victory. If only every problem could be solved with a little thought and conversation.

HUD FILLED IN the rest of the team about the break-in at Dane Trask's home. "There was no heroin in that house when we searched it," Knightbridge said. "Lotte would have found it." At the sound of her name, the Belgian Malinois at his side looked up, alert.

"Didn't you say Montrose PD found heroin in that private detective's car?" Dance asked. "Could there be a connection there?"

"Richard Salazar is still in county jail," Hud said. "I checked."

"Maybe the connection is Trask's daughter," Redhorse said. "She had an opiate addiction."

"To prescription painkillers," Hud said. "Not heroin. And she's been clean for years." Painkiller addicts did sometimes turn to heroin for a cheaper fix, but Audra showed none of the signs of addiction.

"Has she been to her father's house since we searched it?" Dance asked. "She probably has a key."

"I don't think so, but I'll ask her." He wanted to protest that Audra didn't have anything to do with this, but he bit back the words. Dance's question wasn't unreasonable. They needed to rule out Audra's involvement if they were going to find the real culprit.

"Have you discovered anything useful in Roy Holliday's records?" Commander Sanderlin asked.

"I've created a time line of his last days, and a list of everyone he noted speaking to," Hud said. "Though he usually identified people only by their initials. I haven't figured out all the names yet."

"Share what you have, and let's see what we come up with," Sanderlin said. "And talk to Audra Trask. Maybe she can shed light on that heroin and where it might have come from."

"HEROIN?" AUDRA STARED at Hud, trying to make sense of this latest development. She'd been pleased when he met her at her home after work, anticipating a pleasant evening together that was sure to take her mind off her troubles, at least for a few hours. Then he'd shattered that happy fantasy with the news that someone had broken into her father's home. "Dad didn't do drugs," she said. "Ever. He would never have had heroin in his home. Someone else must have put it there after he was gone."

"I have to ask, just to make sure I'm covering every base." Hud looked as upset as she felt. "Have you been in your father's house since he disappeared?"

Did he think *she* had put heroin in her father's house? That she had anything to do with heroin? The words hurt more than she would have thought possible. "No," she said. "I wouldn't do that."

"I never thought it was you," he said. "But I had to ask."

Maybe that was true, but the knowledge didn't lessen the sting of his words. As a DEA agent, would he always think of her as a former addict—someone who might relapse at any moment? She forced her mind back to the break-in. "Was anything stolen?" she asked. "My dad had some really nice electronics, and guns and stuff that I think were valuable."

"It doesn't look like they took anything," Hud said. "But I think they were looking for something." The pained expression returned. "They really trashed the place. They slashed cushions and emptied out cabinets. I can give you some names of companies who will go in and deal with the mess after the police release the scene. It's not something you'll want to tackle yourself."

She tried to picture the scene he described, but couldn't. Her father was an orderly man who shelved his books by topic and arranged his furniture at ninety-degree angles. The idea of someone destroying that order hurt. "What were they looking for?" she asked.

"I was hoping you'd have an idea," he said. "What

would your father want to hide? Did he keep money in the house, or important documents?"

"He has a safe in the bedroom closet for that sort of thing."

"The safe wasn't disturbed."

"Then I don't know what to tell you."

"He must have run into veterans in the Welcome Home Warriors group who struggled with addiction," Hud said.

"Yes. And he always tried to help them." The way he had helped her.

"What if they wouldn't accept help?"

"I think he kicked people out a couple of times, if they were disruptive. But no one recently. At least not that I knew about."

He pulled her close, and she didn't resist. "I hate to always be the bearer of bad news," he said.

"Better you than someone I don't know." She pulled back enough to meet his gaze. "I know you have to ask hard questions sometimes," she said. "But I want you to trust me."

"I trust you," he said. "And I don't say that lightly."

She nodded and moved out of his embrace. "All right, then. You can help me cook supper, then we'll watch a movie. We both need a break from this case." She needed to step back from worry and stress for a while and focus on being young and navigating a relationship with a man who could be both lover and accuser.

THE NEXT DAY, Hud focused on reviewing Roy Holliday's files yet again. He couldn't shake the feeling there was something in them that was vital to this case. Was MR Mitch Ruffino, TDC's vice president in charge of the Montrose facility? If so, then the reporter had contacted him, most likely in relation to research Holliday was doing on Dane Trask. Had his questions led Ruffino to believe Holliday knew something damaging to TDC or Ruffino himself? But what was that information?

Holliday's body had been dumped in the same area where construction debris had been illegally deposited. Though the Rangers had investigated TDC as the possible culprit, they had found nothing to link the company with the debris. But why had Holliday's body been left there?

He looked again at the list of evidence they had collected from the dump site. The one item that stood out to him was the children's drawing, signed "Max." Hud pulled up the scan of the drawing of a boxy, broad-shouldered figure scrawled in red crayon, with an oversize head and a wild tangle of black hair. He had seen no connection to the Dane Trask case or TDC when the drawing had been discovered at the dump site, but now it seemed so clear. A small child had made this drawing. TDC was constructing a new elementary school, which would also be the site of Audra's new day care and preschool. Was Audra the link between TDC and the dump site? And even Roy Holliday's murder?

He printed a copy of the scan, then checked in with the commander. "I'm going to show this to Audra

Trask," he said. "It's possible it was made by one of her students."

"Didn't Beck check the roster of her school for a student named Max?" Commander Sanderlin asked.

"Yes, but maybe this is a student's sibling," he said. "Or maybe Max isn't the student's name, but the name of the person in the drawing."

"Better check it out," Sanderlin said.

He found Audra in her office, frowning at her computer screen. The frown didn't fade when she turned to greet him. "Another student was withdrawn from the school this afternoon," she said. "The mother said it was because she had made other arrangements for care, but I worry it's the influence of the news stories."

"I'm sorry to hear that," Hud said. "Let's hope the media finds something else to latch on to soon."

"I hope so. In the meantime, what can I do for you?"

He pulled a chair up to her desk and sat, then handed her the copy of the child's drawing. "What do you make of that?" he asked.

"Um, it's a copy of a kid's drawing?" She squinted at the name in the corner. "We don't have a Max here at the school. Where did you get it?"

"It was found at an illegal dump site on public land. I'd like to show it to your teachers. Maybe one of them will recognize it as their student's work."

"All right." She studied the paper again. "Some of the three-year-olds and most of the four-year-olds can write their names," she said. "We'll start with the fours."

"That's Jana Keplar's class, isn't it?" he asked, following her from the office and into the hallway."

"Yes. The threes are with Trina Guidry."

Jana was reading a story to the assembled children when Audra and Hud entered and took a seat at the back of the room, Hud perched awkwardly on a tiny blue plastic chair. Every child swiveled to stare at him, and though Jana continued to read for several minutes, she finally gave up and closed the book. "Addison, you and Mia get the modeling clay, and we'll work on shapes and numbers as soon as I'm done talking with our visitors."

She joined Audra and Hud near the door. "It's very disrupting, barging into my classroom this way," she said.

"This will only take a few seconds," Hud said. He passed over the drawing. "Do you recognize this?"

She glanced at the drawing and handed it back. "No. I've never seen it. What's this about?"

"I'm just trying to figure out who drew this," he said.

"Why?" Jana turned to Audra. "Are you involved in another crime? What is wrong with you?"

Audra gripped Hud's arm and dragged him from the classroom. She all but vibrated with anger, her face flushed, her eyes blazing. He was glad he wasn't the object of her ire. "I'm going to advertise for a new teacher starting today," she said as she headed down the hallway once more. "I don't care how much her parents and students love her, I can't work with that woman one day longer than necessary."

She stopped outside a door painted bright orange, with a large 3 on the front. "This is Trina Guidry's classroom," Audra said. "I think you'll like her."

The young African-American woman who looked up when they entered wore a colorful scarf around her long dreadlocks and a dress printed with sunflowers. She and a group of children were gathered around a wire cage against the wall. "Come on in," she said. "The children and I were just feeding the guinea pigs."

"Their names are Gilda and George," a little girl said.

"Officer Hudson just needs a few seconds of your time," Audra said. "The children can tell me about George and Gilda while you're talking."

"George is the boy!" said a child with a great many freckles.

Trina followed Hud to the door. "Is something wrong?" she asked.

"Nothing's wrong," he said. "I'm just hoping you know who did this drawing." He handed her the paper.

She smiled. "Oh, I think that's one of Mason's drawings," she said.

"Mason?" He squinted at the scrawled letters at the bottom of the page. "This looks like it says Max."

"Yes. Some days he likes to be called Max. Would you like to meet him?"

"Yes."

"Mason, come say hello to Officer Hudson."

The boy with the freckles hurried to join them. Hud squatted down until he was eye-level with the child. "Do you remember drawing this?" he asked.

Mason/Max pushed out his bottom lip as he studied the drawing. "I remember," he said. "It's a man who is singing and playing the guitar. And the people who are listening really like the song."

Hud nodded. Questioning a three-year-old was more challenging than interrogating a thirty-year-old. "Do you remember when you drew it?"

Mason shook his head.

"Do you remember where you drew it?"

Mason's quizzical look clearly communicated that he thought this was a dumb question. "No."

Hud looked up at Trina. "Do you know?"

"I really don't know. We draw almost every day. It's one of the children's favorite things to do."

"Are we going to draw now?" Max asked.

"In a little bit," Trina said.

Max handed the drawing back to Hud. "You can keep this," he said, then ran to rejoin his classmates around the guinea pigs.

"What do you think?" Hud asked Audra when they had left the classroom.

"I can't imagine how that drawing got from here— if it was done here—to that dump site," she said.

"Who are Mason's parents?" he asked. "What do they do?"

"His father is a soldier, currently stationed in Afghanistan. He's been there for six months now, I think. His mother is a stay-at-home mom with three other children, all a little older than Max."

"I'll have to dig a little deeper."

"This dump site—is that where Roy Holliday's body was found?"

"Yes," he said.

"Then do you think this drawing ties someone here at the school to his murder?"

"No. The drawing was found long before Roy died."

She put a hand to her chest. "You don't know how relieved I am to hear that. I hate anyone thinking I or anyone else here had anything to do with that poor man's death."

"I'm going to go back out to the site and look around more," he said. "It's officially a crime scene, now that Roy's body was found there, so that halted the cleanup efforts."

"Can I go with you?"

Her request startled him. "I want to see it," she said.

"Why do you want to see it?"

She pressed her lips together, then said, "I guess I want to see if I have any sense that my father has been there."

"It's not a part of the park he's been spotted in. It's not even in the national park, but on public land just outside the park."

She looked away. "I'm being silly, I guess. I just— I know he's out there and I wish I could reach out to him, some way."

"I don't think he's there," Hud said. "But you can go with me. Maybe you'll see something I haven't." And maybe it would help her to deal with everything she was going through right now. If he could do that for her, it would be something.

By THE TIME Hud's Ranger Brigade SUV bumped down miles of rocky dirt road and pulled over in the shade of a large rock formation, Audra felt as if she'd been transported to another planet. She stepped out of the vehicle into an alien landscape of gravel, sagebrush and red-and-gray rock monoliths casting long shadows over the mostly barren ground. The sun beat down with a blinding brilliance, and heat radiated off the rock, alleviated only a little by a hot wind that tugged at her clothes and whipped her hair back.

"This is certainly remote enough," she said. "How far are we from the highway?"

"Only about two miles," he said. "But yeah, it's remote. That's why whoever did this was able to get away with it for so long."

"This" was mountains of trash dumped haphazardly across the landscape in front of her—broken concrete, pieces of lumber, rocks, sections of drywall and sheets of plastic, tipped out like sand from a child's bucket onto the beach. "It must have taken months to haul all of this out here," she said, following him along a path marked by yellow flags into the debris field. He had warned her in the car to only walk where he walked and to avoid touching anything.

"It wouldn't have taken that long," he said. "A few big dump trucks could have probably deposited all of this in only a few days."

She put up a hand to shield her eyes and stared toward an area cordoned off with yellow-and-black plastic tape. "Is that where they found Roy Holliday?" she asked.

"Yes."

She tried to recall Holliday's face, but her encounter with him had been so brief she had no recollection of him. "Where did you find Mason's drawing?" she asked.

"Over there. There's still a flag marking the spot." She stared in the direction he was pointing and was able to make out a bit of blue plastic on the end of a wire stuck in the ground. "It was mixed in with some rock and broken concrete."

"It doesn't make any sense that one of my students' drawings ended up out here." She shook her head.

"I haven't figured that out yet, either," Hud said. "But I'm working on it. But what about this place—do you think this is someplace your father would come?"

She turned slowly, until her back was to the garbage, and she had a view of barren hills, piles of rocks and the blue, blue sky. "Dad liked places like this," she said. "Wild places. Open places where he said he had room to think."

"My dad used to take me camping, too," he said, moving up beside her. "Well, my mom, too. I sometimes think she liked camping and the outdoors even more than he did. But we always camped in the woods, near water. We fished and canoed and hiked. It was fun, but I was always glad to get home to my room and my stuff and my friends."

"Oh, yeah, that was me, too," she said. She squatted and sifted the gravelly soil through her fingers. "When I was little, Dad would take me camping, and he would always tell me to stop and look around my feet. He'd ask me to describe what I saw. No matter how many times he had me do that, I was always amazed at everything that was going on down at ground level." She studied a small beetle who carried a piece of leaf across the ground in front of the toe of her right shoe. "That was Dad—looking at the little details. Seeing what other people ignored." She looked up at Hud. "I'm afraid that's what got him in trouble. He noticed something TDC, or someone else, didn't want him to notice, and he had to run for his life."

Hud held out his hand. She took it; his fingers were warm and strong as he pulled her to her feet. "I'm worried about Dad," she said, continuing to scan their surroundings, as if she expected her father to step out from behind one of the piles of debris. "Even though I always thought he could do anything, I'm not so sure. Maybe he can survive in the wilderness, but what else is he up against? Is it TDC or someone else?" She turned and put her hands on Hud's shoulders. "I want you to meet Dad. I think you'll like him."

"But will he like me?"

"I'd make him like you."

He kissed her, and she closed her eyes and surrendered to the kiss. It didn't quell the nervousness that made her insides feel as if she'd swallowed broken pottery, but it helped. It made her feel a little safer and a lot less alone.

Then Hud shoved her violently to the ground. Pain shot through her as her knees slammed against the rocks, and her eyes blurred with tears. Then she heard the explosive sound of gunfire. Hud eased off her and pushed her toward a boulder. "Get behind that rock," he ordered.

She lurched toward the rock shelter on her hands and knees, heart in her throat, terror driving her forward. Once behind the rock, she peered out to see Hud scooting backward toward her, pistol in hand. Then he was beside her, firing up into the rocks above them, and the only thought that pushed past her fear was, *I don't want to die.*

Chapter Twelve

The sniper was aiming at them from a ledge high above, bullets striking close enough to explode shards from the rock they were hiding behind. A single shooter, Hud thought. He must have been up there awhile, watching them. But why stake out this remote location? And why wait until they were about to leave to fire on them?

"Who is up there?" Audra whispered. She was pressed against his back, so close he could feel her trembling.

"I don't know." He hadn't noticed any other vehicles on the way in, though someone could have parked farther up the road and he wouldn't have known. It would take a while to hike up to that ledge, though.

Audra shifted behind him. "I've got my phone to call for help," she said. "But there's no service."

"There's no service anywhere here until you get to the marina at Blue Mesa Reservoir," he said.

"Then we're trapped here." She sounded calm. Maybe she was in shock. He shifted to glance back at her and went cold all over.

"You're bleeding." He put a hand to her cheek, which was wet with blood.

She put her hand over his, then probed the spot. "It's not a bullet," she said. "Just a piece of rock, I think."

He dug out his handkerchief and pressed it over the wound. "Hold that there," he said. "Press down to stop the bleeding."

"You're bossy when there's danger." But she said the words with a hint of a smile. He wanted to pull her close, but forced his attention back to the sniper. Whoever was up there hadn't fired for a while. Was he repositioning to get closer? Would he try to come up behind them?

"What's he doing up there?" Audra asked.

"I can't tell." Should he try to draw the shooter's fire? Carefully, he picked up a rock and tossed it into the bushes about six feet away. Nothing. Their assailant wasn't falling for that trick.

He kept his gaze fixed on the spot the shooter had been firing from, but could detect no movement. The spot was too far away for him to have any hope of hitting the guy with a pistol. He should save his ammunition in case the sniper moved in closer. But Hud needed to know the shooter's position. Taking aim at a spot just below the ledge, he fired. A puff of dust marked his shot, but only silence answered.

"Maybe he's gone," Audra said.

Or maybe he was moving closer. Moving in for the kill.

Hud considered his options. The cruiser was

parked on the road, about two hundred yards away, across open ground. There were a couple of piles of boulders between here and there that offered some shelter, and his body armor gave him a better chance of surviving a hit, provided it wasn't a head shot. But that would mean leaving Audra alone here, where she was possibly more vulnerable.

In the car he had a rifle, a shotgun and a Taser, plus more ammunition. And water—he was conscious of being very thirsty. The sun beat down on the rock, radiating heat. They couldn't stay here too many hours before they might be in real trouble. The rifle would even the odds a little if he could retrieve it. He also had a radio that might or might not enable him to call for help, depending on how well the repeater system worked here. When he was here with other members of the Rangers before, it hadn't worked at all.

They could wait awhile and hope someone else came along—but that wasn't very likely. The Rangers all had assigned duties, none of which would bring them to this remote location today, and this wasn't a place tourists were likely to wander.

"How long do we just sit here?" Audra asked.

"A little longer," he said. "Listen for anyone moving around up there." Even the stealthiest person was bound to scrape a foot in the loose gravel at some point.

At first, all he heard was his own breathing, but as that slowed and quieted, he became aware of the wind rattling the branches of a dead piñon and stirring the tall stems of wild lettuce and bear grass. A lizard scurried over the boulder they hid behind, tiny claws gripping the rock, the drag of its tail a whisper in his ear.

Audra shifted, probably trying to get comfortable. "I don't hear anyone," she said.

Neither did he. "We should wait a little longer." Move too soon, and it could cost them their lives.

Audra lowered the handkerchief from her face. "I think the bleeding has stopped," she said.

"That's good. I'm glad you weren't hurt worse."

"I'm tougher than I look." Another slight smile, which made him feel momentarily light-headed. No matter what else happened, he couldn't afford to lose this woman.

He sat up straighter, aware of some change around them. "Do you hear that?" he asked.

She raised her head. "Is that a car?"

"I think so." He strained his ears, and the sound of a rumbling engine and tires on gravel grew louder. But the car wasn't coming from the highway—it was traveling from farther up this gravel track. It continued to move closer, growing in volume and speed. He shifted position and could see a small section of the road through a gap between boulders. A cloud of dust appeared, almost obscuring the white SUV it engulfed. Hud couldn't tell anything about the driver through the heavily tinted windows.

As the SUV passed the dump site, it picked up more speed, the back wheels fishtailing in the gravel, great plumes of dust rolling up like smoke from a wet bonfire, until the only clue that a car lay within was the dull red glow of the brake lights as it navigated a sharp curve.

"We should have jumped out and waved," Audra said. "We should have tried to stop them."

"No, it's good that we didn't do that," he said.

"Why not? Maybe they could have helped."

"I think that might have been our sniper," he said.

She gaped at him, then sagged back against the rock. "How can we find out?" she asked after a moment.

"I'm going to go out there. If he's still up there, I'll draw his fire."

She grabbed on to him, fingers digging in hard. "No! You could be shot."

"I don't think I will be. And I'm wearing body armor."

"You don't have armor on your head! Or your legs and arms! What am I supposed to do if you're hurt?"

"It'll be okay," he said. He wasn't at all sure of that, but who else would have been parked down this road? Who else would speed up passing a law enforcement vehicle, to make sure he and the vehicle he was driving couldn't be identified later?

He leaned down and drew the small revolver out of his ankle holster. "Do you know how to fire a gun?" he asked her.

She nodded. "Dad took me to the shooting range. He taught me gun safety and made me practice." She frowned. "It's not something I really kept up with."

"Take this." He handed her the revolver. He'd feel

better knowing she wasn't completely defenseless if something did happen to him.

"All right." Dried blood stood out against her pale cheek, and he could read the fear in her eyes.

He kissed her cheek. "It's going to be okay," he said, and then sprinted out from the shelter of the boulder.

He ran a zigzag pattern toward the next grouping of rocks, shoulders tensed for the bullet he half expected to come. But no shots sounded, and only the rasp of his own ragged breathing accompanied him to his cover.

The next sprint was longer, and the third longer still, but with each one, he gained confidence. Whoever had been firing at them earlier was gone. He reached the cruiser, climbed in and started it, then guided it over the rough ground to Audra's hiding place.

As soon as he stopped the vehicle, she hurried out from cover and into the passenger seat. She leaned back, eyes closed. "I've never been so terrified in my life," she said.

"Yeah." He reached back and pulled two bottles of water from the cooler on the floorboard, and handed one to her. "I need to report this and get some people out here to investigate," he said. "Do you want me to get someone to take you home?"

"No." She opened her eyes. "I'd rather stay here with you."

"I'd rather have you here." For a little while longer, at least, he needed to see her, to know for sure that she was all right.

"Why do you think he left?" she asked.

"I don't know. Maybe he never intended to kill us, only to scare us away. Maybe he got cold feet about killing a cop. Or a woman."

She hugged her arms across her stomach. "Scare us away from what? We haven't figured out anything."

"And someone wants it to stay that way."

THE BLUE AND RED revolving lights of law enforcement vehicles cast eerie shadows across the rock monoliths and sagebrush-covered slopes around the illegal dump site. Spotlights bleached all color from the construction debris and sent long shadows up the sides of the surrounding cliffs. Audra huddled in the passenger seat of Hud's cruiser, a square of cotton gauze taped over the gash a shard of rock had cut in her cheek. The wound ached, and her whole head throbbed, but the EMTs who had arrived with three cruisers of Rangers in response to Hud's call for help had decided she didn't need stitches or further medical attention.

Mostly, she wanted to go home, but she was too afraid to go there by herself. That unknown shooter, firing on them from the hills, had felt somehow personal. As if her enemies—her father's enemies?— wanted her not only disgraced, but dead. And why? Why send a private investigator after her? Why smear her reputation in the newspapers? What had she ever done to hurt anyone?

She had been sitting here for hours, as the last light

faded from the sky, waiting for Hud and Lieutenant Dance to return from their climb into the hills, to the place where Hud thought the person who had fired on them had been hiding. When she saw him walking toward her through the harsh glow of the spotlights she sat up straighter, some of the weight lifted from her shoulders. "What did you find?" she asked when he reached her.

"Someone was up there, all right," he said. "We found some spent brass, some scuff marks. And we found where he parked the car, off the road behind the remains of an old corral."

"He must have driven in ahead of you and waited," Dance said.

"He let us wander around here for a while before he ambushed us," Hud said. "Was he waiting to see what we would do?"

"Maybe he was moving into position." Dance addressed Audra. "Who knew you were coming here with Hud this afternoon?"

"No one," she said. "We met up after work, and I didn't tell anyone where I was going."

"We talked about it at your school," Hud said. "Maybe someone overheard."

She considered this. "We were standing in the hallway. There wasn't anyone else there."

"Could someone in a classroom have heard us?" Hud asked.

"Maybe, if they were listening at the door. But who would do that? And why?"

"I don't know, but I think we'll look into your staff a little more closely," Dance said.

The idea of any of the people on her staff—all women—climbing up into the hills and trying to kill her and Hud with an assault rifle was so absurd, she wanted to laugh. But her cheek and her head hurt too much to allow laughter. "Do what you have to do," she said. "But I don't think this was someone on my staff."

"Any other ideas who might want you out of the way?" Dance asked.

Who might want me dead? She suppressed a shudder. "What about the private detective—Salazar?" she asked. "Maybe you should talk to him again, and ask about the person who hired him."

"We've been trying to track down Lawrence," Dance said. "Salazar has been cooperative, but Lawrence hid his tracks well. But we'll keep digging."

She nodded. "I'm so exhausted, I can't even think."

"Hud can take you home," Dance said. "We've done all we can here for now."

She would have said she was too keyed up to relax, but once in the comforting darkness of the cruiser, the radio murmuring softly in the background, neither she nor Hud speaking, she drifted off, unconscious until he gently woke her in the driveway of her home.

"I think I should stay here tonight," he said.

She touched his cheek, feeling the rough stubble from where he needed to shave. "I think you should," she said. They could comfort each other and escape, for a little while, all the hurt that crowded in too close during the day.

HUD ENDED UP spending much of the weekend with Audra, working at a laptop on her sofa while she did paperwork at the kitchen table. Though the events of the past week were never far from her mind, the weekend felt like a return to normalcy, or rather, a new normal, one where Hud was part of her everyday life.

By Monday morning, her cheek had turned an ugly purple, though the cut itself was small enough she hoped it wouldn't leave a scar. "How do you feel?" Hud asked, examining the wound after she emerged from the shower.

"It's pretty sore. And I'm vain enough to be self-conscious about it."

"You're still beautiful." He brushed back her hair and kissed her bruised cheek.

She wrapped her arms around him, wishing they had time to go back to bed. Loving him was the only thing that made her forget herself and her troubles these days. But life didn't stop just because she wanted it to. "Do you think I'll frighten any children?" she asked.

"Oh, probably not too many." Laughing, he danced out of the way. He had her smiling through breakfast, and by the time she arrived at work, she was feeling more optimistic. As horrible as last week had been, today was bound to be better.

Brenda hadn't arrived yet when Audra pulled into the parking lot, the admin's reserved space still empty. So she was surprised when she walked into the administrative suite and saw the door to her office open. She stepped inside and stared at Jana, who sat in Audra's chair, the desk drawers pulled open. "What are you doing?" Audra demanded.

Jana looked up. "What happened to you?" she asked. "You look terrible."

"Never mind about me." Audra moved forward and put her bag and purse on the desk. "What are you doing going through my desk?"

"I wasn't going through your desk. I was looking for a pen."

Audra grabbed a pen from the mug on the corner of the desk. "Then why didn't you look here?"

"Thanks." Jana tugged on the pen, but Audra refused to release it. "Why were you going through my desk?" she asked again.

"I have to get to class." Jana stood and tried to move past, but Audra blocked her.

"You're not going anywhere," Audra said. "You're fired."

"You can't fire me."

"I can. Now you have ten minutes to collect your things and leave."

"What are you going to do with my class?"

"I'll take it this morning, then I'll call in a sub." She had a short list of moms who would fill in as needed, in exchange for a break on their children's tuition.

"You can't do this," Jana said, her face reddening. "I'll sue."

"I caught you, red-handed, riffling through my desk," Audra said. "That's grounds for dismissal."

Jana glared, and Audra wondered if she was going to have to call the police to escort the woman off the premises. But after a few tense seconds, Jana stormed out of the office. Audra followed, watching as Jana collected her purse and a tote bag of books and papers and other items from her classroom. Then the older woman marched out.

Brenda was coming in as Jana was leaving. "Is Jana sick or something?" she asked, watching Jana's red Toyota screech out of the parking lot.

"Jana is fired," Audra said. "I came in this morning and caught her riffling through my desk."

"What?" Brenda's eyes widened. "Did she take anything?"

"I don't know." Audra tried to remember if she had anything in her drawer worth taking. "But going through my personal belongings is grounds for dismissal."

"What are you going to do about her class?"

"I'll take it this morning. Call the subs until you find someone who can come in this afternoon. Don't tell them why we need them—just that we have a teacher who's going to be out for the next few days. I'll draft an ad for a new teacher."

Chapter Thirteen

Audra spent the morning with the four-year-old class. Being with the children, focusing on them, calmed her. Jana had planned a science lesson about plants, with examples of bark and ferns and leaves for the children to feel and examine, then they read a story about animals that lived in the forest, and drew pictures of trees. By the time the substitute showed up to take the children to the lunchroom, Audra was feeling more relaxed. She decided to walk to a nearby park for lunch and enjoy the warm weather.

The letter was waiting on Audra's desk when she returned from lunch. A fine linen envelope, with the embossed return address of the Superintendent's Office of the Montrose School District. Stomach churning, she slit open the envelope and unfolded the single sheet of paper:

Dear Ms. Trask,

This letter is to inform you that your contract with the school district is now declared null,

*according to Article 17b of your contract with
us. We will no longer require your services as
director of a day care and preschool facility
in conjunction with Canyon Creek Elementary
School.*

Her eyes blurred as she scanned the following lines
of legal jargon. She set the letter aside, took a deep
breath, then picked up the phone.

"Ms. Arnotte is unavailable at the moment," the
woman who answered the phone at the attorney's office said. "May I take a message?"

"This is Audra Trask. I just received a certified
letter informing me that the school district is canceling the agreement for me to manage the day care
and preschool at their new Canyon Creek Elementary
campus. I need to know if they can do that, and what
we can do to fight it."

"I'll give her the message."

Audra ended the call. The initial numbness upon
reading the letter was fading, replaced by a growing
rage. She punched another number into the phone.

"Superintendent's office. This is Maeve."

"Maeve, this is Audra Trask. I need to speak to
Superintendent Wells."

"Superintendent Wells is not in. But I was told if
you called to tell you that the decision is final and
there's nothing we can do to help you." And then she
hung up before Audra could say another word.

Audra was still staring at the phone in her hand
when it rang. "Hello?"

"Audra, this is Cheryl Arnotte. What's going on?"

"I received a certified letter from the school district. Let me read it to you." She read the letter. For a long moment, Cheryl didn't say anything. "How can they do this?" Audra asked. "We have a contract. That's legally binding, isn't it?"

"They're invoking the morals clause. They have the right to cancel the contract if they feel your behavior jeopardizes the reputation of the school district."

"I haven't done anything. Certainly nothing that would violate a morals clause."

Another long pause.

"What is it?" Audra asked. "Do you think I've done something immoral?"

"Not necessarily immoral," Cheryl said. "But your name has been linked with a murder, and my girls tell me there have been law enforcement officers at the school several times recently. That concerns me as a parent, so I can understand how it would concern the school district, too."

"I'm not a suspect in any crime," Audra said. "The police have questioned me, but only as a possible witness."

"A school's first mission has to be to protect the children in its care," Cheryl said. "I think most courts would consider them justified in exercising an abundance of caution."

"Are you saying you agree with what they've done?"

"I'm saying I understand what they've done. I can file an appeal if you want me to, but I would caution against it. I don't think you'll win, and it could be very expensive."

"Do you plan to withdraw your children from Canyon Critters?" Audra asked.

"Certainly not right away. But when the new school opens, it will be so convenient for me to drop off all the children at a single location. I'm sorry, but I'm just being honest with you."

Audra didn't answer. What did you say to a remark like that—thanks for nothing?

"I understand this must be extremely upsetting for you," Cheryl said. "Don't rush to do anything right now. Wait a few days and consider your options. Then get back to me."

What options would those be? Audra wondered after she ended the call. She had put everything— all her savings, all her credit, all her experience and training—into Canyon Critters. Once the new school opened, she doubted many parents would opt to stay with her. The new location was much nearer TDC Enterprises, where many of them worked. Those with older children, like Cheryl, liked the convenience of having all their children on one campus. Others simply wouldn't want to be associated with someone as notorious as Audra Trask.

She couldn't have said later how she made it through the rest of that day. She closed her office door and pretended to work on her computer, but she lost long minutes staring vacantly into space. She wanted to call Hud, but he was working. And she didn't want to be that needy girlfriend who was always calling to cry on a man's shoulder. She kept telling herself this wasn't the worst thing that could have happened to her. She wasn't dying of cancer. No one she loved had died. So many people had dealt with true tragedies. She was only in danger of losing a business she had poured her life into.

Okay, so maybe that wasn't cheering her up. But she wasn't aiming for cheerful. She just had to find a way to keep going. To stay standing until she could figure out a better way forward.

After work, she got behind the wheel of the car, intending to drive home, cry her way through a long, hot shower, then put on her pajamas and eat her feelings with a pint of ice cream. Or a bottle of wine. Or both.

Instead, she found herself driving to what would have been the future home of Canyon Critters Daycare and Preschool. Late-afternoon light bathed the construction site in a soft golden glow, warming the red stone of the emerging buildings to the same shade as the surrounding rock. The construction crews had left for the day, and she parked and walked across the gravel that would one day be a paved parking lot.

She had stood in almost this same place the day of the groundbreaking. She and her staff had brought all the children to watch the ceremony, the little ones excited at the prospect of a field trip and by the sight of all the construction machinery ringing the area. Audra had stood with the other people involved as the ribbon was cut and the first shovel of dirt removed. Then a backhoe had moved in to start digging the foundation. She could still see the children, wide-eyed and thrilled to watch the big machines. Some of them had drawn pictures and waved them like little banners.

"Oh!" The cry escaped her involuntarily as another memory surfaced, clear as if she had just witnessed it. Mason stood behind the ropes that separated the children from the construction zone, a crayon drawing in hand. The wind had caught the drawing, whipping it from his hand and into the path of the backhoe. He had cried and had to be restrained from running after it, but had soon been distracted, watching the backhoe bite into the earth, imitating the movement with several other boys, roaring like a monster.

The paper with his drawing had fluttered away, soon buried in a shower of construction debris from one of the backhoes.

HUD WAS WALKING out of Ranger Brigade headquarters when Audra's RAV4 pulled into the lot. He jogged over to the vehicle as she turned into a parking space. "What is it?" he asked. "Is something wrong?"

"I just remembered something," she said. "Something important."

"What is it?"

"It's about that drawing—the one Mason did. I know how it ended up in that dump site."

"Come on." He took her arm. "Let's go inside so the whole team can hear."

Beck, Dance, Reynolds and Redhorse, as well as the commander, were still at headquarters when Hud returned with Audra. "Audra has some new evidence for us," Hud said, and led the way to the conference room.

He set up the recording equipment as the others piled in, then sat across from Audra at the table. "Tell us what you know," he said.

"The day of the groundbreaking for the new elementary school, we took the Canyon Critters students to see the ceremony," she said. "The kids were really excited about seeing all the heavy equipment. Some of them were carrying drawings they had made that morning. I remember Mason dropped his drawing. The wind picked it up and carried it into the path of a backhoe, which dumped some rocks and concrete and stuff on it."

"You're sure about this?" The commander leaned toward her.

"Absolutely sure," she said. "I was at the construction site this afternoon and the memory came back to me, clear as if it had just happened."

"What were you doing at the construction site this afternoon?" Redhorse asked.

Her expression grew more troubled. "I received a letter from the school district this afternoon informing me they were canceling my contract for the new day care and preschool on the elementary school campus. I was upset and wanted to see the place one more time."

"Can they just cancel a contract like that?" Hud asked.

"They invoked a morals clause. Apparently, they

think my involvement in this case could be damaging to their reputation."

He wanted to vent his own rage at this turn of events, but had to maintain his composure for the tape and in front of his coworkers. "I'm sorry to hear that," he said. "I imagine that was upsetting."

"I'm not so upset now," she said. "That drawing proves TDC dumped that construction debris illegally on public land."

"I interviewed the construction supervisor for the elementary school," Jason Beck said. "He showed me receipts for dumping all the construction debris and talked about how committed TDC is to green practices."

"People lie and receipts can be faked," Reynolds said.

"This ties TDC to the dump site," Sanderlin said. "But it doesn't prove they actually dumped that debris. A contractor could have dumped it illegally."

"It's not enough to get a warrant to inspect their accounts," Dance said.

"Even if we got a warrant, they've probably covered themselves," Hud said.

"How much money do you reckon they pocketed by charging for waste disposal and dumping it on public land instead?" Beck asked.

"It could be as much as $250,000," Dance said. "Construction debris costs about $500 a ton to dispose of, and the national forest techs estimated that dump site has five hundred tons or more."

"They gave the school district a big discount on

the construction of the school. This was a way to get a little back."

"It's pocket change for someone like TDC," Audra said. "They lost more paying those fines to the EPA."

"They're contesting those fines," Sanderlin said. "They say Dane Trask faked the reports to get them into trouble."

"My father wouldn't do something like that," Audra said.

"Then maybe Trask caught them lying and threatened to blow the whistle," Hud said. "They threatened him or his family and he decided to run away and hide out instead."

"Then why not go to the press or someone at the EPA to begin with?" Redhorse asked. "Why disappear and leave a lot of cryptic reports for other people to figure out?"

"Because that was too dangerous," Audra said. "I know my father. It would have to be something really risky to keep him away this long."

"It would help if we had someone inside TDC," Beck said.

"Dane Trask was on the inside, and it didn't help him," Hud pointed out.

"Can we put more pressure on Mitch Ruffino?" Dance asked.

"We can question him," Sanderlin said. "But that doesn't mean he'll tell us anything. And I imagine he has plenty of lawyers to make sure he doesn't say anything to incriminate himself or the company."

"Let's try," Dance said.

"I'll see if I can reach him at his office," Hud said. "We can go over there now."

He expected an assistant to put him off, but when he identified himself and asked to speak to the TDC vice president, he was put right through. "I was just about to call you people," Ruffino said, without any preamble.

"Oh? What can we do for you?" Hud asked. He looked up and found everyone else in the room leaning forward in their chairs, listening intently. Now he wished he'd thought to put the call on speaker.

"We've had a break-in at TDC headquarters," Ruffino said.

"When did this happen?" Hud asked.

"Very early this morning. And I'm sure the culprit is Dane Trask."

Chapter Fourteen

Mitch Ruffino met Hud and Commander Sanderlin in his office on the sixth floor of the TDC office building, four miles outside the national park boundary. TDC's vice president had a fringe of snow-white hair around a bald spot and an expression that hinted at chronic indigestion or a dissatisfaction with life in general. "I don't know why it is taking you people so long to stop this man," Ruffino began as soon as they were admitted to his office. He stood behind a massive desk, arms crossed, radiating belligerence. "You're supposed to be an expert group, but this one man is making you look like clowns."

"You're working late this evening," Sanderlin said, ignoring the outburst.

"It's not unusual for me to work late," Ruffino said. "It's a requirement for the job, but one I don't mind. I do some of my best work after most people have left the office."

"Tell us about this break-in," Sanderlin said. "You said it took place early this morning?"

"At 3:52 a.m., according to the time stamp on the security footage," Ruffino said.

"Did you call the sheriff's department to report the break-in?" Sanderlin asked.

"No. I was going to call you people, but you contacted me first." He frowned. "Why was that?"

"We wanted to ask you some questions," Hud said.

"Those will have to wait until after you deal with this break-in."

The commander moved in closer to Ruffino, his lean figure towering over the VP. "Why did you wait so long to report the crime?"

Ruffino looked away. "We needed time to review the security footage, and we wanted to determine what might have been taken."

"And in the meantime, you were conducting business as usual," Sanderlin said.

"Of course. We are a multinational company with many projects to oversee."

Sanderlin didn't hide his annoyance. "Which means any evidence we might have gathered if you had reported the break-in immediately has been compromised."

"That's your problem, not mine."

"What was taken?" Hud asked.

"Thankfully, nothing. But the footage shows he was clearly looking for something."

"We'd better have a look at the footage," Sanderlin said.

Ruffino picked up his phone. "Send Larry in with the video footage," he said.

Seconds later, as if he had been waiting right outside the door, a middle-aged man with thinning blond hair and wide blue eyes entered, a compact disc in hand. "I have the footage right here, Mr. Ruffino," he said.

"This is Larry Keplar," Ruffino said. "He's head of our IT department."

"You're working late today, too," Hud said. "Is that usual?"

"Mr. Ruffino asked me to stay, to talk to you," Keplar said.

"Any relation to Jana?" Hud asked as Keplar fed the disc into a computer drive.

Keplar looked up, clearly startled. "Jana's my wife," he said. "How do you know her?"

"She works at Canyon Critters Daycare," Hud said.

"Yeah, she does." He turned his attention back to the computer. "Okay, it's going to play right now."

Hud and Sanderson leaned in closer as a grainy black-and-gray image appeared on the screen. A time stamp in the corner clearly showed 3:52 and that day's date. The figure—little more than a shadow at times—moved around a room, opening and closing file drawers, then riffling through a desk. At its clearest, the image appeared to be a slender man, over six feet tall, dressed in dark clothing. The search took about ten minutes, then the room was empty again.

"Is this the only footage?" Hud asked. "Do you have any of the man entering the building or searching anywhere else?"

"No, we don't," Ruffino said. "But how much more

do you need? He's clearly not supposed to be snooping around like that at almost four in the morning."

"How did he get in?" Hud asked.

"Obviously, he used a key card," Ruffino said. "Anything else would have set off an alarm."

"You didn't deactivate his card after he left?" Sanderlin asked.

"Of course we did. But he must have gotten hold of another one."

"Run it again, please," Hud said. He watched the figure carefully, but could find no identifying marks. The man kept his head down, obscuring his features.

"What makes you think this is Dane Trask?" Sanderlin asked when they had reviewed the footage a second time.

"Who else would it be?" Ruffino asked.

"It could be almost anyone," Hud said. "The image quality on this footage is so poor we can't make out his features—not to mention, he's avoiding looking toward the camera. It's like he knows it's there."

"Exactly!" Ruffino said. "Dane Trask knows our security system and he knows how to avoid it. It's why we don't have footage from anywhere else in the building."

"Where is this footage from?" Hud asked.

"It's from the file room on this floor," Ruffino said.

"He avoided all those other cameras, but didn't avoid this one?" Sanderlin asked.

"He was too focused on looking for whatever it is he wanted," Ruffino said.

"Do you have any idea what he was looking for?"

"I don't know. Maybe confidential documents or proprietary information he thought he could use against the company. He's made it clear he wants to destroy us."

Hud thought it was clearer that TDC wanted to get rid of Dane Trask, but he remained silent, watching the video repeat. He turned to Keplar. "What about motion sensors? Don't you have those?"

"We do, but—" Keplar looked to Ruffino.

"They were shut off," Ruffino said. "Which is another reason it had to be Trask. He knew how to bypass our system."

"Didn't Trask work as an engineer?" Hud asked. "How would he have known how to bypass your security system?" He looked at Larry again. "I would imagine it's a pretty sophisticated system."

"Well, yes," Keplar said. "I don't really know how he could have bypassed it."

"Clearly, the man is not an idiot," Ruffino said. "And he was somehow able to bypass our system."

"We can't identify the man and nothing was taken," Sanderlin said. "There's not a lot we can do."

"That is Dane Trask!" Ruffino stabbed a finger at the screen. "At the very least, he's trespassing."

"I suggest you file a complaint with the Montrose County sheriff," Sanderlin said. "This is their jurisdiction, not ours."

"But the Ranger Brigade is in charge of the hunt for Dane Trask," Ruffino said. "This is your problem. I want to know what you're going to do about this."

"We're continuing our investigation," Sanderlin said.

Ruffino leaned toward them, finger upraised as if he intended to poke Sanderlin in the chest. He refrained. "You've questioned Trask's daughter, haven't you?" he asked. "She must know something."

"Ms. Trask has cooperated fully with our investigation," Sanderlin said.

"And what has she told you? Does she know where her father is hiding? Has he told her what he has against us? How he plans to smear our name?"

"The details of our investigation are confidential," Sanderlin said. He turned to Larry. "We'll need a copy of that footage," he said.

"Of course." Larry ejected the disc and handed it to Hud.

"Why do you think Dane Trask has targeted TDC Enterprises?" Sanderlin asked.

"Because he embezzled from us and he's trying to deflect the blame," Ruffino asked. "He has the mistaken belief that by trying to make us appear in the wrong, it will lessen his own guilt."

"What, exactly, is he trying to make you appear wrong about?" Hud asked. "Was it just the false reports about the levels of contaminants removed in the mine cleanup, or is there something else?"

"Dane Trask faked those reports." Ruffino's voice rose. "We did nothing wrong."

"What about the construction debris that was illegally dumped on public land?" Hud asked. "Could some of that come from TDC?"

"Is that what Trask is saying now?" Ruffino asked. "It's absolutely untrue. And I believe one of your

men already talked to our construction superintendent about that and we were cleared."

"Where were you Friday, about six thirty?" Hud
asked.

Ruffino glared at him. "Why are you asking?"

"Where were you?"

"I was here, at the office. I told you, it's not un-
common for me to work late."

Ruffino didn't have to have been the sniper who
fired on Hud and Audra. It would be more his style
to hire a professional to do the job for him.

"I expect you to report back with your findings,"
Ruffino said as they turned to leave.

Sanderlin made no answer. When he and Hud were
back in the cruiser, he asked, "What do you make of
that security camera footage?"

"I would expect a company like TDC to have better quality security cameras," Hud said. "I noticed
on the way in, they have cameras at the entrances, in
the lobby and in the elevators. Even if the intruder
knew to take the stairwells, and for some reason TDC
doesn't have security cameras there—which would
be a big oversight—I don't see how he avoided being
caught on film everywhere but that one spot."

"Maybe he really was able to bypass the system,"
Sanderlin said.

"I'm not convinced that was Trask in the video,"
Hud said. "And for all the guy was going through
drawers, it didn't look to me like he was searching
for anything in particular. The whole thing felt staged
to me."

"Staged for TDC, or staged for us?"

"Staged for us. I think Ruffino wanted an excuse to get us to his office so he could try to find out whatever we know about Trask." He frowned. "He seemed particularly focused on Audra." That really bothered Hud. Could Ruffino and TDC be behind the bad press Audra had suffered lately?

"Take a closer look at that video footage and see if you find anything significant," Sanderlin said. "From what I've learned about Dane Trask, he might very well be capable of bypassing a security system. But if he got into TDC headquarters to steal something in particular, I don't think he would have abandoned the task after ten minutes."

"What are you going to do about Ruffino?" Hud asked.

"Nothing for now. But we'll keep a close eye on him."

Hud would be keeping an eye on Ruffino, too—and looking for anything that might link him to Audra's woes. An attack on her was beginning to feel very personal.

AUDRA WAITED UP for Hud to return from TDC headquarters. She hadn't objected when he had suggested he spend the night with her again. She felt more vulnerable lately than she had in years, and having him with her eased her fears somewhat. Plus she was anxious to know what he had learned from Mitch Ruffino.

It was after eleven when his cruiser pulled into the

driveway. She met him at the door, but only offered a hug and a kiss, resisting the urge to pepper him with questions. He shed his gun and utility belt at the door, then went into the bedroom, where he removed his body armor and uniform and changed into sweats from the bag he had brought with him. "Are you hungry?" she asked. "I could make eggs or something."

"Somebody ordered in pizza at the office," he said. "So I'm good." He opened his arms. "Come here."

He hugged her tightly, and she wondered at his ardor. "What's wrong?" she asked, searching his face for some clue to his emotions.

"I can't prove anything," he said. "But I don't think it's a bad idea for you to be wary of anyone and anything having to do with TDC."

She pulled away. "What did you find out?" she asked. "Did Mr. Ruffino say anything about me?"

"He asked if we had questioned you. He said he was sure you knew something about your father and his 'plans.' He's definitely convinced your dad has it in for the company—and maybe for him personally."

"But he didn't threaten me or anything, did he?" Her stomach trembled at the thought.

"No. But he's a man who's used to having a lot of power and using it to get what he wants."

"Did my dad break into TDC headquarters?"

Hud put an arm around her shoulders, and together they moved toward the living room. "Someone was on a security tape they showed us. There was a lot suspicious about the footage, which I won't go into. But there's no way to tell it's your dad. I don't think it is. I think the whole thing was an excuse to get us to his office so Ruffino could try to find out what we know. He ended up disappointed."

"TDC could have paid that private investigator to dig into my background," she said. "Then they leaked my past to the news media. And I wouldn't put it past them to have put pressure on the superintendent to drop me from the school contract. They donated the land for the school, and that probably bought them some influence." She sank onto the sofa. "Or I could be imagining all of it."

"What can you tell me about Jana Keplar?" Hud asked.

"Jana?"

"Her husband, Larry, works for TDC. Did you know that?"

"I think she might have mentioned it. Lots of the parents who have children in the school work for TDC. It's one of the largest employers in the area. Did you meet her husband?"

Hud sat beside her. "Yes. He's head of the IT department. He's the one who gave us the security footage. I thought he looked nervous, and was clearly watching Ruffino for cues." He rubbed her back. "What happened with you and Jana? Did you fire her?"

"Yes. We never saw eye to eye on the whole bullying issue, or anything else, really. But this morning, I got to my office a little early, and she was there, going through my desk." Anger rose as she remembered the scene. "I caught her red-handed and she didn't even try to deny it. Instead, she accused me of overreacting and tried to change the subject. Obviously, she wasn't happy about being fired, but I stood up to her."

"Who will teach her class?" he asked.

"I have a couple of moms with teaching experience who have agreed to fill in. And an ad will start running tomorrow for a new teacher." She turned to meet his gaze. "Why? Do you think she's the link between me and TDC? Or her husband?"

"I don't think anything. I was going to warn you to be cautious, since she was working for you. Now that she's not around, it shouldn't matter."

"When I got home this evening, I had a message on my phone from Brenda, my assistant. She said Jana is already talking bad about me all over town. She also said she heard a rumor that the school district has awarded Jana the contract for the new day care and preschool."

"That has to hurt," he said.

"I'm getting past hurt and moving on to anger. Now I wonder if Jana might be the one who hired the investigator and told the media about my addiction history." She hugged a pillow to her chest. "Or maybe I'm being paranoid and it's all coincidence. No one has made me a target. It's just my turn for bad luck."

"It's not all bad," he said.

"No." She tossed aside the pillow and put her head on his shoulder. "Meeting you has been good. Whatever happens, I'm not going to regret that."

THE NEXT MORNING, Hud ran through the video footage from the TDC break-in again and again. The intruder entered the room at 3:52, went straight to the first tall filing cabinet and opened the drawer. He did a quick scan of the contents, pulling out one file, then putting it back before moving on to the next drawer. He performed a similar scan of each drawer, moving quickly, as if searching for something obvious that he did not find. He didn't read the contents of any file folder, and unless he was a speed reader, wouldn't have had time to read the title of each folder. He pawed through the drawers of a desk and looked through two other file drawers. At 4:03, he exited the room.

Enlarging the images was no help in identification, proving that the image was blurry as well as grainy and ill lit. Which begged the question of how the intruder had managed to determine anything about those files, since he wore no headlamp and carried no flashlight. From the height of the door, Hud was able to determine that the intruder was approximately six foot two—Dane Trask's height. He wore gloves and a knit hat, a long-sleeved dark jacket, possibly a windbreaker, and dark slacks, possibly jeans. He kept his head down so that it was impossible to tell much about his features. Even Audra probably wouldn't be able to identify her father if he was, indeed, the man in this video.

He closed the file and sat back in his chair. "Any luck?" Beck asked, looking up from his own desk, across from Hud's.

"Nothing. I need to talk to Larry Keplar again." He stood. "If anyone is looking for me, I'll be at TDC headquarters."

Chapter Fifteen

Hud didn't go into TDC's building, but parked near the entrance to the employee parking area and waited. He had been there an hour when Larry Keplar strolled out and headed toward the back row. Hud started his engine and drove slowly, arriving just as Keplar was unlocking the door of a white Jeep. Hud rolled down his window. "Hello, Larry."

"Hello, Officer." Keplar glanced toward the building, as if checking to see if anyone was watching.

"I wanted to talk to you about that security video you gave me," Hud said.

"Is something wrong?" Keplar swallowed, his freckles dark against his very pale skin.

"I just need to clarify some things."

"Now? Here?"

"It doesn't have to be here," Hud said. "Is there someplace else you'd like to meet?"

"You know Newberry's?" Keplar fiddled with his key fob.

"Sure," Hud said. "Why don't we meet there?"

"Okay." Keplar jerked open the driver's door of

the Jeep and dived in. Hud waited for him to pull out, then followed him to Newberry's, a combination convenience store/tavern/gas station/post office near the lake. Keplar parked at one end of the gravel lot and led the way into the dim interior lit by neon beer signs and smelling of ancient cigarette smoke, even though smoking had long been banned in bars.

He took a seat at a booth along a side wall and Hud slid in across from him. When a middle-aged waitress in a pink sweatshirt and jeans appeared to take their order, Keplar asked for Bud Light, and Hud ordered a Coke. A country tune began playing somewhere near the back of the bar, and Larry slouched lower in his chair. He had discarded his tie on the drive over and rolled up the sleeves of his white dress shirt. "What did you want to talk to me about?" he asked.

"I was wondering if you figured out how your intruder bypassed the security system," Hud said.

"No." He looked up to accept the beer from the waitress and took a long pull. "I never met Dane Trask, but people say he was really smart. Still, I didn't find anything showing the system had been messed with. That sort of thing usually leaves some kind of electronic fingerprint, so to speak."

"And you didn't find anything?"

"Nothing. No blank spaces or destroyed data or time gaps or anything."

"Nothing suspicious at all?"

Keplar took another long sip of beer. He wiped at a drop of moisture on the table with his thumb.

"Mr. Ruffino told me not to talk to the police or the press," he said.

"When was this?"

"After you left yesterday."

Hud sipped his drink, letting the silence expand between them. He had a sense that Keplar wanted to tell him something. "You're not obligated to tell me anything," he said. "But there's no need for anything you do say to get back to Mr. Ruffino."

The door opened, and two men came in. Keplar started, then relaxed as they took seats at the bar. Not fellow employees, Hud guessed. "The only thing odd was, the camera lens in the file room looked as if it had been smeared with Vaseline," Keplar said.

"Do you think the intruder covered the lens with the Vaseline?" Hud asked. That would explain the blurry, distorted image.

"Maybe. Maybe he wanted us to know he was there—that's why he let himself be filmed in the file room—but he didn't want anything that could identify him."

"Walk me through everything that happened after the break-in at headquarters," Hud said. "Your part in the whole aftermath."

Keplar finished his beer and set the glass down on the coaster. "I got to work yesterday morning at nine, and Mr. Ruffino called me to his office maybe half an hour after I got in. He said he thought someone had been in the file room the night before and I needed to check all the security footage."

"Did he say what made him think someone had been in the files?" Hud asked.

"No. And I didn't ask. When the VP tells you to do something, you do it."

"So you looked and found the footage showing someone in that room at 3:52, is that right?"

"Right. I noticed what poor quality the footage was, so I went to the file room to check the camera. It looked like someone had smeared something sticky—like petroleum jelly or something—all over the lens. They had tried to clean it off, but there was still some residue."

"And there wasn't footage showing an intruder anywhere else?" Hud asked. "You checked all the other feeds?"

"Yes, and the entrance logs."

"Did any of the other cameras show signs of having been covered or tampered with?"

"No."

"Had anyone entered the building around that time? Say, between midnight and 3:52?"

"The system showed that one person checked in at 3:45. They used a generic card—the kind we give to vendors or visitors. They have to surrender them at the front desk. Each generic card is coded with a number we can match to the guest and vendor registry, but this card wasn't linked to anyone. In fact, it was a brand-new card, made just the day before."

"How do you make a card?"

"It's a little machine—the same kind they use for hotel key cards. You swipe the blank through the reader and it codes the metallic strip to unlock one or more doors. If someone forgets to turn in their key, we can void that key remotely."

"Has that happened lately? Someone forgetting to turn in their key?"

"No. I checked."

"So you don't have any idea who used the card?"

"I assume it was the intruder—Mr. Ruffino is sure it was Dane Trask." Keplar frowned. "But anyone using the card should have shown up on the security feed for the front entrance—that's the entrance they used."

"I know you said you didn't find any irregularities. But if you were going to bypass the system, how would you do it?" Hud asked.

"You can buy technology that will interfere with the system," Keplar said. "Disrupt the feed for a few seconds. If it was only a few seconds, it would be harder to detect."

"Where do you buy something like that?"

"There are lots of places online."

"Anything else odd you noticed?"

"Not really."

Keplar had been focused on his system's failure, not the failure of the intruder to find anything worth taking in a quick perusal of files in an almost dark room. "I have to get home now," Keplar said. "My wife will be wondering where I am."

"Your wife worked for Audra Trask," Hud said.

Keplar froze in the act of reaching for his wallet. "She did. Audra fired her."

"Did your wife tell you why she was fired?"

"What does that have to do with anything?"

"What did she tell you?"

"She said Audra resented her because Jana knows more about kids and how to run a day care. She had her own day care center in Kentucky, where we used to live."

"Audra told me she caught your wife going through her desk."

"I don't know anything about that." He pulled out his wallet.

"Do you think your wife would do something like that?"

He counted out bills and laid them on the table. "Look, Jana is a great person. She loves kids, and she loves teaching. She was pretty torn up about having to leave her day care center behind when we moved here."

"Why did you move here?"

"This job is a tremendous opportunity for me. TDC is huge, and this was a big promotion for me, not to mention a big pay increase. Jana's business was profitable, but only barely. It didn't make sense to stay in Kentucky and pass up a chance like this."

"So she took the job with Canyon Critters."

"Yeah. She has all this experience, and she loves kids. But it's been hard on her. Audra is pretty young, and she's not interested in hearing advice from someone like Jana. But Jana can't help wanting to give advice. I thought things would settle down after a while, but I guess they didn't."

"I heard your wife was awarded the contract for the new day care center," Hud said. "The one that was initially given to Audra."

"I'm not even going to comment on that." He slid out of the booth. "I really do have to go now."

Hud finished his Coke, thinking about their conversation. Larry Keplar had moved across the country to take a better-paying job with TDC. He had a wife who resented the move, and probably a bigger mortgage on top of that. He depended on his paycheck, and he depended on TDC for that paycheck. That hadn't stopped him from going against Mitch Ruffino's orders not to talk to law enforcement, but it had made him nervous and not inclined to dig very deep into the mystery of that security footage.

As for Jana's clash with Audra, maybe it had nothing to do with TDC. Coincidences happened all the time in real life, one of the things that made solving real crimes tougher than they usually were on TV.

AUDRA SAT AT her desk and read the article someone had anonymously forwarded to her, a story from the local newspaper's website. Successful Daycare Operator from Kentucky Awarded New Contract for School Facility, declared the headline. The article announced that Jana Keplar, former owner of Sunshine Kids Daycare in Paducah, Kentucky, had been awarded the contract to operate a day care and pre-school on Montrose School District's Canyon Creek Elementary campus. "I'm excited for this opportunity to bring a truly top-tier facility to local families," Mrs. Keplar said.

More paragraphs followed detailing Jana's experience, with no mention of her former association with Canyon Critters Daycare, and no mention of Audra Trask. Audra supposed she ought to be thankful for that.

She closed the file, then squeezed her eyes shut against a fresh flood of tears. Despite the brave front she had put on for Hud, she was struggling not to sink into depression. This morning, after Hud left for work, she had lain in bed, thinking about the days when she could just take a pill and zone out. For a few seconds, the idea had been very tempting.

But she was never going to do that again. She was going to be strong and fight her way through this.

How would her dad handle this? He had been her role model for most of her life, more so than her mother, even. What would he do now?

She hesitated only a moment before she booted up her computer. When it was ready, she looked up a phone number, then punched it into her phone. "TDC Enterprises," a man answered.

"I need to speak to Mitch Ruffino," she said. "This is Audra Trask." She was going to arrange a meeting with Ruffino and have it out with him, face-to-face. She could almost hear her father speaking in her head. "When you need to address a problem, skip the middleman and go straight to the top."

MITCH RUFFINO HAD always impressed Audra as the sort of man who was so concerned with the impression he was making and so focused on always asserting his power that he could never unbend or so much as crack a smile with anyone he felt was beneath him. At the few TDC functions she had attended with her dad, Ruffino had kept himself apart from the others, a ruler overseeing his subjects, watchful for any missteps or slights he might pounce on. Now that she faced him in his office, she saw nothing to change the opinion of him.

She made a point of looking him in the eye and returning scorn for scorn. She had spent her young life disabusing people of the notion that she was weak merely because she was diminutive.

"So you're Dane Trask's daughter." Ruffino looked her up and down. "You don't look anything like him."

She had her father's eyes and chin, if not his stature. And she had his obstinacy. She also had a taste for risk that, while it had gotten her into trouble more than once, in this situation might come in handy. She ignored the chair Ruffino gestured to and stood in front of his desk, her hands resting lightly on this barrier between them. "You and your company have harassed me enough," she said. "You need to stop right now or I'll be forced to take action."

A muscle in his jaw twitched, and his nostrils flared. She watched, the way she might watch a snake, ready to leap out of the way before it struck. "I don't know what you're talking about," Ruffino said.

"I'm talking about the private detective you hired to dig into my private life," she said. "Mr. Salazar."

He had schooled his emotions enough not to react

to this, but he shoved back from the desk and stood also. "You can't come in here threatening me."

"I just wanted to deliver that message. I'll leave now." She turned and headed for the door.

"Stop!"

She halted, but didn't turn. His feet shuffled on the thick carpet until he was standing in front of her. "Don't go," he said. "Let's talk."

All graciousness now, he led her to a seating area to the left of the desk, a low sofa and two chairs with a glass-and-steel coffee table. He took the sofa and she sat on the edge of one of the chairs, her purse in her lap. She had a can of pepper spray in there, one her father had given her a couple of years ago, when she'd moved into her own place. She didn't even know if it was any good anymore. Did things like that expire? Mainly, she hoped she wouldn't need to use it.

"Tell me what you want," Ruffino said.

"I told you. I want you to leave me alone," she said. "And leave my father alone. Stop lying about him stealing that money. And stop this ridiculous lawsuit. A judge is just going to throw it out anyway." She was taking risks again, but she was here, so why not go for broke? Her father had also taught her to always ask for what she wanted. If people said no, you really weren't any worse off than you had been before.

Ruffino's eyes narrowed. "How do you know your father didn't steal that money?"

"Because he wouldn't. He didn't need money."

"Everyone needs money. You really are naive if you think they don't."

"My father didn't need more of your money. He made a good salary in his job, and he didn't have any debts."

"That you're aware of."

She shook her head. She really knew very little about her father's financial situation, but she knew his character. "Right now he's living in the wilderness, eating campers' leftovers," she said. "Does that sound to you like a man who cares a great deal about money?"

"No. That sounds like a desperate man. Possibly a deranged one."

She didn't argue; rather, she stood again. "I've told you what I want, so I'll leave now. I know you're a busy man."

"You won't leave until I'm ready. Sit down."

She started to ask if he was going to sit on her to keep her from going, but decided against that. Instead, while she didn't sit, she waited. Something else her father had taught her—don't rush to fill a silence. Other people will often tell you things if you wait.

Ruffino didn't disappoint. "That little school of yours," he began. "I'm sure you could use money to expand and grow."

She looked at him, still silent.

"I see you know the value of not speaking," he said. "That's good. I'm willing to pay for you to continue to keep quiet."

Keep quiet about what? she wanted to ask. But that was the risk she had taken—the gamble that appeared to be paying off. Ruffino thought her father had revealed to her some secret he didn't want anyone else to know. He was offering to pay her to keep quiet.

"Talking to the wrong people could get a person in a lot of trouble," she said vaguely.

Ruffino's scowl deepened. "And I'm telling you that not talking could make you a very rich young woman."

"Did you try making this offer to my father?" she asked.

His expression didn't change. "You strike me as much more intelligent than your father."

She took that to mean yes, he had tried to bribe her father, and Dane had turned down the money, or whatever else Ruffino had offered.

"Yes," she said. "I'll take you up on your offer." This was a risk, too. What was she going to do if he handed over a big stack of cash? Would that be enough proof for the police to move in?

"You have to do something for me first," Ruffino said.

Her stomach rolled. "What's that?"

"You have to hand over the proof. Your father said he had proof hidden in a safe place. Obviously, he left it with you."

She swallowed hard. "How do I know you'll hold up your end of the bargain if I give you the proof?" she asked.

He smiled, revealing surprisingly white teeth. "You'll just have to trust me."

Chapter Sixteen

"Given everything Larry Keplar told me, I think it's possible that Mitch Ruffino staged that break-in at TDC headquarters in order to add to the urgency of finding Dane Trask, and so that he could quiz us about what we know about Trask and his relationship with TDC." Hud concluded his summary of his interview with Keplar to his fellow Rangers half an hour after he parted company with Keplar.

"Ruffino isn't the man in that video footage," Beck said. "That guy is taller and thinner than Ruffino."

"I think he hired someone to break in, but I think Ruffino set it all up," Hud said. "He would have known—or could have found out—how to make the visitor's key, and he could have given the guy a device to interfere with the security cameras at the entrances, elevators and hallways. He could have smeared something on the camera lens in the file room and wiped it off later. And he was the one who made the decision not to call in the Montrose sheriff and to wait all day, until any trace evidence would have been obliterated, before calling us."

"The biggest thing that stands out to me is that, while the intruder made a show of looking through the files, he wasn't actually looking for anything," Redhorse said. "He didn't turn on a light, and he only made a cursory search."

"Why even bother with paper files?" Dance asked. "I would think anything important at a business like TDC would be on the computer."

"They have paper copies of a lot of signed contracts, surveys and land plats," Hud said. "But even then, I don't think they would keep anything incriminating or valuable in a file room that is accessed every day by dozens of people. Which is another reason this whole thing was a ploy to try to find out what we know."

"Ruffino is worried about something," the commander said. "How do we find out what?"

"Dane Trask knows something," Dance said. "I don't know why he doesn't come right out and tell us."

A knock on the door of the conference room interrupted them. "Come in," Commander Sanderlin said.

Stacy, one of the civilian employees, came in. "Audra Trask is here to see you, Officer Hudson," she said. "I told her you were in a meeting and she said the commander should probably hear what she has to say also."

"Send her in," Sanderlin said.

A few moments later, Audra entered the room. Before she spoke, Hud could tell she was agitated. Her eyes were bright, her color heightened. "I just came from a meeting with Mitch Ruffino," she said. "He tried to bribe me. He thinks my father gave me some kind of evidence relating to TDC Enterprises—something Ruffino doesn't want made public."

Hud stared at Audra, trying to absorb what she had just said. "You went to see Ruffino?" he asked, aware of the anger behind his words but unable to stop himself. "By yourself?"

She raised her chin, defiant though pale, and in that moment his love for her hit him like a punch to the gut. Everything she had endured these past few weeks would have sent a lot of people hiding under the covers, but she was still fighting, refusing to give in. "Somebody leaked the information about my battle with addiction," she said. "Somebody hired that private investigator to look into my background. TDC has been doing everything they can to discredit my father, so it's not unrealistic to believe they're going after me now—maybe as a way to get to my dad. One of the things my father taught me, way back when I was struggling with bullying, was to turn and confront my tormentor. It throws them off guard and forces them to face their actions. And it lets them know you're not going to let them get away with what they're doing."

"So you decided to confront Ruffino." Sanderlin spoke, and Audra turned toward him.

"He's in charge of TDC's operations here, and he was my father's boss," she said.

"Why don't you sit down." Beck stood and pulled out a chair for her. Hud wished he had thought of it first.

Audra sat, purse in her lap. She was still pale, but composed.

"I think we should get your statement on record," Sanderlin said. He nodded to Dance, who went to a corner cabinet and started the recording equipment. Sanderlin recited the date and time and introduced Audra as the speaker. Then he turned to her. "All right. Tell us everything that happened."

She looked around the table at each person, ending her survey with Hud, her gaze steady and, he thought, pleading with him to listen and not be angry. He forced himself to relax and nodded. "Go ahead," he said. "We want to hear what you have to say."

"If you've seen the papers, you probably know that someone leaked a story about my having struggled with drug addiction in the past," she began. "It was an addiction to prescription painkillers, and I went into rehab and haven't had any problems since. So, old news, obviously put out there to hurt me and, I believe, to hurt my father. I already knew someone had hired a private detective to look into my background, and I suspected it was TDC Enterprises, since they've kept up a stream of bad publicity about my father since he disappeared. Then, probably as a result of that publicity, I lost the contract with the school district for the new day care center and preschool that's supposed to share a campus with the new elementary school. TDC is building that school, and I suspect they have some influence with the district. Rumor has it they gave the district a big price break on construction costs. Then, Officer Hudson showed me a child's drawing that was found at a site on public land where someone illegally dumped construction debris. I remembered seeing one of my students with that drawing at the groundbreaking ceremony for the new school. That linked TDC to the illegal dump site—which was also the place where Roy Holliday died." She paused and took a deep breath. "And then someone shot at me and Officer Hudson when we visited the dump site. At first I was terrified, then I was angry. Everything kept coming back to TDC. So I called the vice president of the company, Mitch Ruffino, and asked to meet with him. He agreed right away, which I guess was my first clue that something was up."

She took a sip of water from the cup Hud had slid over to her. No one else said anything, all eyes on her. Hud could think of a lot of things he wanted to say— he wanted to tell her what a risk she had taken, going to TDC. If everything she believed about them was true, confronting them could have put her life in danger. It might still have. But he forced himself to keep quiet. The damage was done, and he recognized the bravery that went along with her foolishness. Maybe this would help them break open this tough case.

"Have you found out anything else about the person who shot at us at the dump site?" she asked.

"They didn't leave anything behind that's helped us identify them," Dance said. "And TDC still denies they had anything to do with the construction debris dumped there. The drawing is a pretty tenuous link, since the argument could be made that it was dropped by the child somewhere else."

"We've had people at the site around the clock since then and haven't had any incidents," Redhorse said.

"What happened at the meeting?" Sanderlin prompted.

"We met in Ruffino's office at TDC. I told him I wanted him to stop harassing me," she said. "At first, he tried to deny that he'd done so. But when I told him if he didn't stop the harassment, I'd take action, his attitude changed."

"What kind of action?" Dance asked.

"I meant legal action, but I think Ruffino thought I meant something else," she said. "When I tried to leave his office, he told me not to go. Then he offered to pay me to keep my mouth shut."

"Shut about what?" Sanderlin asked.

"I don't know," Audra said. "But I didn't tell him that. I played along. I told him I knew talking to the wrong people could make trouble for him. He said if I kept quiet, I could be a very rich woman."

"Did he offer a specific amount?" Redhorse asked.

She shook her head. "No. I asked him if he made my father the same offer, but he didn't answer. I took that to mean yes, he had tried to bribe my dad. Maybe he'd threatened him, too, and that's why my dad felt he had to disappear."

She fell silent, as if contemplating her father in danger. "What happened next?" Hud prompted.

"Ruffino said in order to get the money, I had to

hand over the proof my father had left with me. I had no idea what he was talking about. My father didn't leave me anything—certainly not 'proof' of anything. But I played along. I agreed to give him what he wanted in exchange for a lot of cash. And I agreed to meet him Thursday at seven to make the exchange." She looked around at them. "I thought maybe you could be there and record the conversation and maybe I could get him to say or do something incriminating. Something that would prove my father is innocent."

Hud had to bite the inside of his cheek to keep from telling her agreeing to such a meeting was a terrible idea and that there was no way they would risk a civilian like this. But that was only because of his feelings for her. With any other witness, he would have seen this as a breakthrough in the case. The others certainly recognized it.

"Are you sure your father didn't give you anything?" Reynolds asked. "A computer disk? Or one of those flash drives, like he gave Cara Mead?"

She shook her head. "I've been thinking and thinking, but there's nothing. He hasn't even contacted me since he left."

"I always thought that was because he was trying to protect you," Hud said. "To keep you out of whatever mess he'd gotten himself into."

"Whatever the mess is, I'm in it now," she said. "And I want to do everything I can to help."

"Where is this meeting supposed to take place?" Dance asked. "Ruffino's office?"

"No. He suggested we meet at the construction site for the new elementary school. He said it wouldn't look suspicious for either one of us to be there."

"That's good," Knightbridge said. "It will be easier to keep an eye on the situation out in the open, not in his office."

"We can fit you with a recording device and a microphone so we can listen in," Dance said. "And we'll have people nearby if we need to intervene."

"Can you coach me on what to say to get the information you need from him?" she asked.

"We can do that," Sanderlin said. "Though I'd say you did pretty well with him so far, making him think you have what he wants."

"Did Ruffino give you any idea of what he's looking for?" Redhorse asked. "Did he specifically mention a flash drive or notes or something like that?"

"No," she said. "I don't think he knows what he's looking for. He said my father told him he had 'proof' in a safe place. Apparently, Ruffino has decided that means my dad gave it to me. But he hasn't given me anything. I swear if he had, I'd hand it over to you. Whatever it is, it must be pretty incriminating."

"Then why didn't your father hand it over to law enforcement?" Jason Beck asked. "From what we know about him, he doesn't strike me as someone who'd be afraid of a man like Ruffino."

"I know," she said. "I don't understand any of it."

"He must have been persuaded that he or someone he cared about was in grave danger," Redhorse said.

Everyone looked at Audra, and a chill ran through

Hud. "We can't do this unless we can be sure Audra is safe," he said.

"We need to be prepared for Ruffino to want to move to another location once he meets her there." Redhorse said.

"I agree," Sanderlin said. "If Dane Trask left because Ruffino threatened him, or threatened Audra, it had to be a serious threat. Ruffino wants Audra to believe he'll be satisfied with paying her off, but I don't believe it."

"You're saying he'll try to kill her," Beck said.

Audra gasped, and Hud leaned over to put his hand on her arm to steady her. "I think Carmen is right," he said. "It's possible Ruffino—or someone he hired—may have killed before."

"What do you mean?" Audra asked. "Who?"

"I don't have solid proof yet, but I've been going through Roy Holliday's computer files," he said. "The day before he was killed, he had a note to contact MR. His phone records show a couple of calls to a private number with a local exchange. That could be Ruffino. I'm waiting on confirmation of that, but I think it's possible Holliday uncovered something suspicious and confronted Ruffino with it."

"And he was murdered to keep him quiet," Knightbridge said.

"I think it's very possible," Hud said. "We've linked TDC to the illegal dump site where Holliday was dumped. And someone fired on me and Audra the day we visited the site, which is yet another reason to believe Audra is in danger."

"How did the sniper know you would be at the dump site?" Dance asked.

"We talked about it in the hallway at the day care center." Hud turned to Audra. "Jana Keplar could have overheard us and told her husband or someone else at TDC. Ruffino might even have recruited her to keep an eye on you."

Audra nodded. "Maybe that's why she was going through my desk the day I fired her."

"Did anyone follow you here?" Hud asked.

She shook her head. "I headed back toward the school when I left TDC, but when I was almost there, I realized I had to tell you about this. I didn't notice anyone following me here."

"If they were very good, you probably wouldn't have noticed," Beck said.

"I really don't think anyone followed me," she said.

"Let's hope they didn't," Dance said.

"Ruffino thinks you have something your father gave you that proves Ruffino or TDC or someone connected with the company did something illegal," Sanderlin said. "Until he gets his hands on that evidence, you should be safe."

"Should" wasn't good enough for Hud. "Maybe she's safe for now," he said. "But once she hands it over, she'll be in real danger."

"We'll be there to protect her," Dance said.

Audra had gone very still, but now she took a deep breath, the fire back in her eyes. "I want to do this," she said. "I want to stop these people. Maybe then my father can come home."

AUDRA HAD LEFT her meeting with Ruffino shaking, and it had taken a while after she had arrived at Ranger Brigade headquarters for the shaking to stop. She could tell that Hud had been angry at first, upset that she'd taken such a risk, but she hoped her explanations had eased his mind. He seemed calmer, though he didn't say anything until the two of them stood in the headquarters parking lot, next to her car. He kept a hand on her arm, his body tense. "You don't think I should do this," she said.

"It's too risky," he said. "You shouldn't have confronted Ruffino by yourself. Not without talking to me first."

"Why not?" she asked. "I didn't go in there thinking he was going to bribe me. I went to confront a bully, in a public place, with plenty of other people around. I had to let him know I wasn't going to let him intimidate me anymore. That was my battle to fight, not yours."

He slid his hand up to her shoulder and looked into her eyes, his expression so intense it sent a shiver down her spine. "You don't have to fight those battles by yourself anymore," he said. "I can help you—if you'll let me."

She had to look away. It was either that or let him see how much he was getting to her. "I'm not used to leaning on other people," she said. She had worked so hard to learn to stand on her own feet, to not depend on drugs, or her parents, or anyone else.

"Leaning on others doesn't mean you're weak," he said. "And I want to help you."

"And I love that about you." She allowed herself the luxury of enjoying the warmth and strength of his hand on her shoulder before she shrugged it off. "But try to look at this as if you weren't my friend— as if you were one of those other officers." She nodded toward the Ranger Brigade building. "You've got this really difficult case and I come in and offer you a chance to collect some valuable evidence that might help you solve the case. At the very least, I could get proof that TDC has broken the law. There was something they did that my father found out about, that they don't want known. I'd really like to know what that thing is, wouldn't you?"

"Not if it means you getting hurt."

"I won't get hurt." She softened her tone. He looked so miserable—far more upset about this than she was. Yes, she was afraid, but she was also excited to be able to do something to help, instead of tossing and turning at night, worried and helpless. "I'm going to have you and your fellow officers to protect me."

"Your father didn't trust us to protect him," Hud said.

"Well, that's where the two of us are different. He didn't trust people easily, but I'm feeling a lot more trusting since I met a certain Ranger Brigade officer."

He didn't exactly smile, but his expression lightened. "You know what this means, don't you?"

"No, but I'm sure you're going to tell me."

"It means you have a personal bodyguard, at least until we've settled this with Ruffino."

"Do I get to choose the bodyguard?" she asked.

His eyes narrowed. "That depends. Who do you choose?"

"Oh, I was thinking I might ask Officer Knight-bridge. He's pretty hunky and has all those tattoos."

His fierce glower made her laugh out loud. "I'm sorry," she said, hand to her mouth. "But the look on your face! I think it's a good thing Officer Knight-bridge isn't here right now."

"Where are you headed now?" he asked.

"Home. I'm exhausted."

"I'll be there as soon as I get done here," he said. "And if anything suspicious happens in the meantime, call 911, then call me."

"You're cute when you're bossy." Something about this situation—maybe her own audacity in confront-ing Ruffino in the first place—had brought out her sassy side. Instead of the panic she probably should have been feeling, she was giddy with excitement, and she couldn't help teasing Hud for being so overly concerned on her behalf. At his dark look, she leaned over and kissed his cheek. "It's going to be all right," she said. "You'll see. Between the two of us, we'll figure this all out. We make a great team."

She got in her car and started the engine. Hud was still watching as she drove out of the parking lot. Maybe she wasn't more afraid because she had faith in him to protect her. No, check that. She wasn't afraid because she had more faith in herself with him backing her up.

Chapter Seventeen

Audra called in sick Wednesday and Thursday, pleading a terrible cold she didn't want to pass on to the children. Brenda promised that everything was under control, and Audra spent the majority of both days in a windowless conference room, trying to memorize the instructions Hud and other members of the Ranger Brigade rattled off. She received guidance on the importance of getting Ruffino to say something that would incriminate him or his company. "Play dumb," Lieutenant Dance said. "Make him explain everything to you. Ask him to explain exactly what information he's worried about you having, or how he could possibly be in any trouble, or how he came up with his plan—anything at all to get him talking in detail about what he or TDC did."

"Won't that make him suspicious?" she asked. "Won't he suspect I'm being recorded?"

"Not if you handle it right." Hud patted her shoulder in what she was sure was meant to be a reassuring manner, but only made her worry more. What, exactly, was the right way to face a man who might be a criminal—even a murderer?

"I'm really nervous," she said. "I'm not sure I can hide that."

"Don't hide it," Carmen Redhorse said. "You don't have to pretend to be anyone you aren't. Of course you're nervous. If Ruffino comments on it, it's okay to say you don't trust him, or even that you're afraid of him."

"But what do I do when he asks me for the proof my dad left with me?"

"You're going to give him this." Hud handed her a red plastic computer flash drive.

She stared at the Welcome Home Warriors logo on the front. "This is one of my dad's." Dane had handed them out all the time to remind people of the veterans' group he had founded.

"Right," Hud said. "Cara let us have it." Cara Mead, her father's former administrative assistant at TDC. "It's exactly the sort of thing Ruffino will expect your father to have given you."

"While we're on that subject," Officer Beck said, "the first time we interviewed you, you said you had some of these—some your father gave you."

"I do. But I've had them all for ages. I even dug out every one I could find last night and looked at them. They're all full of my own files."

"You mind if I take a look at them, just in case?" Hud asked.

"Sure."

Hud took the flash drive from her. "I'll keep track

of this until you're ready tomorrow afternoon," he said. "I'll hand it over before you head to your rendezvous at the construction site."

"What's on it?" she asked.

"Variations of the reports that were on the flash drives your father gave to Cara and to Eve Shea," Hud said. "I corrupted the data, so it won't make much sense, but the files look very technical. If Ruffino insists on taking a quick look, they should be enough to fool him. He probably knows his business, but information in his public bio doesn't indicate the scientific background to decipher technical reports."

"Okay." The four of them—Hud, Dance, Beck and Redhorse—looked so confident. Optimistic even. They were counting on her to get this right. "What about the wire I'm supposed to wear?" she asked.

"It's not actually wired to anything." Redhorse picked up a flat cardboard box that had been sitting in the center of the conference table and passed it to Audra. "Everything is wireless these days. We ordered this just for you."

Audra lifted the box and stared at a turquoise-and-pink-quartz amulet on a thick silver chain, with matching drop earrings. "Jewelry?" she asked, confused.

Dance laughed. "The pendant is actually a sophisticated digital recorder. It should pick up everything you both say. It will also transmit to the van where we'll be hiding, so we can monitor the conversation. If we hear anything that sounds like trouble, we'll be right there, with lots of backup."

"You'll also have a code phrase to repeat if you sense trouble and need help," Redhorse said.

"What's the code phrase?" Audra asked.

"We thought we'd let you decide. It needs to be something that sounds natural in conversation," Redhorse said. "Most people choose some comment about the weather, or something like that."

Audra tried to imagine herself having a conversation with Ruffino near the half-built elementary school. "How about 'It's amazing how quiet it is here this time of day'?"

Hud nodded and typed a note into his phone. "That's good, but we won't necessarily wait for that phrase," he said. "If we hear anything we don't like, we'll make our move. The phrase is in case you see something alarming that we can't pick up from the conversation."

She tried not to dwell on what might constitute "alarming."

"Are you clear on what the plan is for tomorrow?" Dance asked.

"I think so. Hud will be at my house with me to get everything set up, and we'll test the recording equipment there."

"Right," Dance said. "Beck and I will be in a van near your house. After we test the equipment, we'll drive to the neighborhood around the construction site and get set up. We'll also have two teams stationed nearby, at least one where they can keep an eye on the site itself."

She nodded. "At twenty 'til seven, I'll drive to the

site and park near the entrance. I'll walk in to meet Ruffino."

"My guess is he'll try to get there first," Dance said. "But if he isn't there, stay inside your car until you see him."

"And after Ruffino and I meet up, we talk, I give him the flash drive and he gives me the money." She swallowed, fear making a knot in her chest. "That's how it's supposed to go, but if he really thinks I know something incriminating about him or TDC, why would he let me just walk away? Why wouldn't he kill me and hide the body, the way he may have done with Roy Holliday?"

"You don't have to do this," Hud said. "We can call the whole thing off now."

"No, I want to do this. I'm just trying to figure out the best way to avoid getting killed."

"That's why we'll be there," Dance said. "If Ruffino tries anything, we'll move in immediately."

"I don't think he'll come alone," she said. "That wouldn't be smart, and he strikes me as pretty smart."

"No, but we'll be prepared to handle anyone he has with him," Beck said.

"But you don't have to do this," Hud repeated.

She took his hand and squeezed. "I think I do have to do it," she said. "It's the only way I see to put a stop to his persecution of me and of my dad."

"I think it's too dangerous," he said.

"It is dangerous," she said. "But if I don't do this, I don't think things are going to get any better. Someone else might even die."

I don't want it to be you. He didn't say the words out loud, but she read them in his eyes. "You ought to know by now that I'm a fighter," she said. "I don't give in easily. I'll be smart, and I won't let Mitch Ruffino get the better of me. My dad and I have that much in common."

He nodded. "I've got your back."

"We all do." Dance put a hand on Hud's shoulder. "Ruffino doesn't know it yet, but he's going up against all of us."

AUDRA STOOD IN front of the mirror in her bathroom and tried to see herself as Mitch Ruffino would—a small woman, wearing jeans and low boots with rubber soles (better for running if she needed to), a pale blue knit shirt with three-quarter length sleeves, and a turquoise-and-pink-quartz pendant with matching earrings. She'd spent some time on her makeup, partly to cover the dark circles under her eyes from sleepless nights since she'd agreed to this risky plan, and partly because she wanted Ruffino to think she was the kind of glamorous, high-maintenance and possibly pampered woman who wouldn't know anything about defending herself. She'd added false eyelashes, heavy liner and dramatic lipstick. She looked ready to go out on the town, not prepared to confront a possible killer. She hoped her appearance would lull him into thinking she didn't suspect he'd double-cross her.

And he would try to double-cross her. She was almost certain of that. Whatever had happened between her father and Ruffino, it had been enough to send her father into hiding. Dane Trask wasn't a man who backed down easily. But Ruffino would have expected Dane to fight back. She imagined a man like him would even be afraid of her father, a former army ranger who was fit and in his prime.

She was counting on Ruffino to not expect a fight from her.

"I've never seen you this dressed up. You almost don't look like yourself."

She turned to face Hud. "I haven't worn this much makeup since a friend and I did one of those glamour photo shoots that were popular when I was in college," she said. "But I'm hoping the glamour will throw Ruffino off guard. If he asks, I'll tell him I plan to go out and celebrate with some of the money he's going to pay me. I'll make him believe the money is all I care about."

Hud put his hands on her shoulders. "You know I don't like this, but I'm proud of you," he said. "And I'm going to do everything in my power to not allow anything to happen to you."

"I know. And that's why I'm able to do this." She touched the pendant at her throat. "Do you know if Dance and Beck are picking up transmissions okay?"

In answer, Hud's cell phone rang. He listened, then said, "Okay," and hung up. "Beck says everything is coming through good, but don't touch the pendant. It creates static, plus you don't want to call attention to it."

"Right." She put her hands at her side. "What time is it?" The day had dragged, waiting for the time that the meeting would start, but now that it was almost here, everything was moving too fast.

Hud checked his watch. "Almost time for you to leave." He walked her to the door. She collected her purse and keys, then turned and kissed him, hard and quick. "I'll be okay," she whispered.

Then she hurried out the door, willing herself not to turn back, not to chicken out. "You can do this," she whispered to herself, but what she heard was her father, telling her the same thing when he dropped her off at the rehab center all those years ago.

She drove to the construction site, keeping to the speed limit and forcing herself not to search for the surveillance van or the Rangers she had been told would be watching over her. There would be officers from the Montrose County Sheriff's Department also, since the school was in their jurisdiction. She turned in at the sign that announced Future Site of Canyon Creek Elementary School.

The school building looked almost complete, only stickers on the windows and a lack of landscaping hinting at work still to be done. Constructed of reddish sandstone blocks, the school blended into the surrounding sandstone boulders, seeming to grow organically from the ground. A low stone wall along the drive separated the pavement from what might be flower beds in the future.

A dark SUV with tinted windows was parked in front of the almost-completed school. Audra turned into the lot, drove a slow circle past the SUV, then back to park in the middle of the entrance drive, the nose of her car facing out. She was blocking the entrance and making it easier for her to drive away. She left the engine running and the keys in the ignition, her purse on the passenger seat, and opened the door.

She was scarcely out of the car before the SUV started up and drove to within inches of her back bumper and stopped. The SUV's driver, a big blond man in a black T-shirt and jeans, got out. "You're blocking the exit," he said.

She faced him. "I am."

A second big man, this one with closely cropped brown hair, dressed in jeans and a black sweatshirt, got out of the passenger seat. "You need to move your car," he said.

"If that's what you want," she said. "I'll leave. Though I came here to meet Mr. Ruffino."

The back door of the SUV opened and Mitch Ruffino emerged. He was dressed casually in khakis and a green polo shirt, as if he were headed to the golf course after this. "Are you in a hurry to leave already?" he asked.

She removed her sunglasses and fluttered the false eyelashes. "I have things to do," she said. "I plan to celebrate big with the money you're going to give me."

"Only if you have what I want." He moved toward her.

She opened her palm to reveal the flash drive. "I think this is what you want," she said.

He reached for it, but she closed her fingers around it once more. "I want to see the money," she said.

"First, we need to search you," he said. "I want to make sure you aren't recording this. My sources say you're pretty friendly with the Rangers."

For a moment, she was sure her heart stopped beating. Her mouth was so dry, she couldn't speak. *You're not afraid*, she told herself. *You're brash and reckless and tough.* She drew herself up to her full height. "You can search me," she said. "But don't you dare get fresh."

Ruffino looked at the blond. The man stepped forward, towering over her, and patted her down. She kept her expression impassive as he groped her, even as she was inwardly cringing against his touch. He took his time going over her body, but he didn't even touch the necklace.

As soon as he took his hands from her, she stepped back.

"You're shaking," Ruffino said. "Why?"

"Because I don't trust you," she said. "My father is missing, and I'm sure it's because of something you did or said."

"Oh no," Ruffino said. "That's all on your father. He went off the deep end and did something stupid. Now he's paying for it. I'm hoping you're smarter."

She thought of a dozen questions she wanted to ask him—what did you do to my father? What did he say to you? But the Rangers had coached her on what to say. "Tell me about the Mary Lee mine," she said.

Ruffino scowled. "What about it?"

"The paper made a big deal out of the fines you had to pay to the EPA. My father was working on that project before he disappeared. I'm worried there'll be more trouble over the mine."

"We took care of all that," Ruffino said. "We got rid of everything that could be a problem. Even the EPA admits it's all clean now. If your father told you otherwise, he's wrong. We were very careful, and everything would have been fine if he hadn't interfered."

"What about this school?" She gestured toward the almost-completed building.

"Everything is fine here, too. We paid off the people who needed to be paid off."

"All those bribes get expensive."

"Don't call them bribes. And we figured all that into our bid."

"Your bargain bid."

He chuckled. "Wells knew it was worth his while to make a big deal over the bargain he was getting. But there are firms who would have done it for half the price we did. Or not done it at all."

She tried to put together this puzzle, but it wasn't making sense. "Did you tell Wells to take the day care contract away from me?" she asked.

"No. He got nervous and did that all by himself. But don't worry. With the money we're paying you, you won't need to work for a long while." He reached into his pocket and she flinched, expecting him to withdraw a weapon. Instead, he took out a slim leather wallet and extracted a check and handed it to her.

She stared at the check, made out in her name for $300,000. "You're giving me a check?"

"We're going to say it's the proceeds from a life insurance policy we provide for all our executives," he said. "Don't worry. No one will suspect anything."

She had expected a suitcase with bundles of cash, or the key to a secret safe-deposit box, or even the number and pass code to a secure offshore account. An ordinary check seemed so absurd. "How do I know this check is any good?" she asked.

"How do I know this flash drive isn't full of nonsense?" He grabbed her wrist, squeezing hard. "No more games," he said. "Time for you to do what I want. My two friends here will make sure of it."

"THAT'S ENOUGH," HUD SAID from the back of the van where he sat with Dance and Sanderlin, eavesdropping on Audra's meeting with Ruffino. "We've got him admitting to bribes. We need to get Audra out of there before she gets hurt."

"Wait," Sanderlin said. "If we handle this right, we can avoid letting Ruffino know we're onto him and avoid exposing Audra to more danger."

"She's not a professional," Hud said. "She shouldn't even be in there."

Sanderlin remained calm. "Listen," he said.

"I don't want just the money," Audra said. "I want the contract for the day care center back."

"You don't need that contract," Ruffino said. "You can do whatever you want with this money, especially if you're smart about investing it."

"It's a matter of pride," she said.

"Your father was proud, too, and it didn't get him anywhere. Trust me, you don't want to work around here."

"Why not?"

"Nothing. I mean, the risks are minimal. People exaggerate the effects of that kind of radiation. Really—you're probably getting more exposure from dental X-rays. That's why we took all that material up to the mine, instead of reusing it at the building site. We were actually making it safer."

"What is he talking about?" Dance asked.

"Radiation?" Audra sounded as puzzled as they were. "How can you be sure it's all gone?"

"We can't be sure it's all gone, but it's nothing for you to worry about. And if you're worried about testing, we've taken care of all of that. Everybody who matters is on our payroll. Everything will be fine. And you need to keep your mouth shut about this, or you'll jeopardize the whole operation."

"How big an operation are we talking about?" Audra asked.

"Good," Dance said. "He went off script, but she's following right along."

"Maybe I want to be part of the operation," Audra said.

Hud and Sanderlin exchanged glances. That definitely wasn't part of the script.

"What could you do for us?" Ruffino asked.

"I own a day care center. Can you think of a better cover? No one would suspect me of anything."

"Interesting," Ruffino said.

"I need to know more," she said. "What role would you allow me to take?"

"I'd have to talk to people above me. But you might be onto something."

"I want—"

But they never got to hear the rest of her sentence. Gunshots—very loud and very close—crackled over the speakers, followed by terrifying silence.

Chapter Eighteen

Audra staggered back, blood from Mitch Ruffino's head sprayed across the front of her shirt. She gaped at the blond man, who had shot Mitch Ruffino. "Why did you do that?"

In answer, he turned the gun on her.

She stared, trying to register in vain what was happening. But some primitive part of her brain—the part desperate to survive—took over. She launched herself over the low rock wall, bullets exploding shards of granite around her. She scrambled on her hands and knees into a culvert, desperate for cover as shouts rang out behind her.

More shots exploded, and it took her a moment to realize the bullets were no longer striking near her. Heart in her throat, she crawled to the edge of the culvert and peered out. Men dressed in black fatigues, with shields and helmets, swarmed the area. The two bodyguards lay on the ground, the blond silent and still, the other in handcuffs, blood running from a wound in his arm.

A white service van skidded to a halt at the front

bumper to her car. The back doors opened and Hud raced out. "Audra!" he shouted.

"I'm over here!" But the words came out so weak he didn't hear her. She managed to back out of the culvert and stand, her knees aching. "I'm over here," she tried again.

A man all in black, face concealed by a helmet, swiveled and pointed a rifle at her. "Don't shoot!" she screamed, and tried to raise her hands in the air. She felt weak and stupid, and tears streamed down her face.

Then Hud was by her side, one arm around her shoulders, holding her up. "Where are you hurt?" he demanded. "We've got to get you to an ambulance."

"It isn't my blood," she said. "It's Ruffino's." She turned to look at the vice president of TDC, who lay faceup and blank-eyed in the glaring sun.

Hud pressed her face into his shoulder. "Don't look," he said.

"The blond man—his bodyguard, I thought—shot him," she said. "One minute we were talking, and then the man just shot him. And he tried to shoot me."

Hud pulled away far enough to look her up and down. Some of the blood was on his uniform now, and the sight made her woozy. "I need to sit down," she managed.

He led her to her car, opened the door and helped her sit in the passenger seat. Commander Sanderlin approached. "How are you doing?" he asked.

"I don't know." It was the best answer she could

give. She was still trying to absorb the idea that she could have been shot, but wasn't.

"The ambulance is on its way," Sanderlin said. "We'll have the EMTs check her out." He was talking to Hud, and she listened with the detachment of someone overhearing two strangers at the next table in a coffee shop.

Sanderlin leaned into the car to address her again. "Do you have the check Ruffino gave you?"

The check—she looked down and realized she was still clutching the check in her fist. It was torn and smeared with dirt and blood. She uncurled her hand and held it out to him.

Hud ran a finger over her bleeding palm. "Your hands are pretty beat up," he said. "Your knees, too."

She looked down and was surprised to see holes in the knees of her jeans, the skin beneath raw and streaked with dirt. "I think it was digging through all that loose rock and concrete," she said. "Trying to get away."

She began to cry then. She couldn't help it. The sheer awfulness of everything that had happened hit her. "I'm sorry," she apologized between sobs.

Hud held her, patting her back, making soothing noises. "It's okay," he said. "It's all going to be okay."

Sanderlin left and the EMTs arrived. They cut away the torn jeans just above her knee, cleaned her wounds and gave her a tetanus vaccination. "You're going to be pretty sore for a few days," one said. "But you should be okay. See your doctor if there's any sign of infection or you start to run a fever."

She nodded. Really, all she wanted right this minute was to take a shower, put on clean clothes, and climb under the covers and sleep away this whole nightmare.

That wasn't going to happen, though. As soon as the EMTs left, Commander Sanderlin returned. "We need to get your statement about what happened," he said.

She wanted to say no. But she had promised to help them, and this was part of helping. "All right."

"I'll drive your car to headquarters," Hud said. "After you've given your statement, I'll take you home."

"That's the most wonderful thing you could have said to me right now." She even managed a smile, though she could still feel the tears walled behind the thinnest of panes of glass, which might shatter any moment. She had never been the weepy type and hated feeling this way now. But maybe this happened to anyone who had seen men shot right in front of her and who had almost died herself.

Ranger headquarters was quiet and almost empty, a sharp contrast to the construction site, which had swarmed with people. Hud led her to the conference room, which was so familiar to her now, then filled a glass with water and set it in front of her. "I'm going to get the recording equipment set up," he said.

Commander Sanderlin came in. "I know you're probably feeling pretty rough right now," he said. "But we need to get all the information you can give us. It's important."

She nodded. "Of course."

"We have the recording of your conversation with Ruffino," Sanderlin said. "But we need you to fill in the visuals—facial expressions, gestures, all the subtext we weren't able to see."

"I'll do my best." She took a drink of water. "I'm still in shock," she said. "I'm not sure if I trust my memory."

"Just do the best you can," Hud said. He sat by her side, and Sanderlin took the chair across from her, on the other side of the table.

"Start by describing everything that happened after you left your house," Sanderlin said. "Then we'll go back over everything and clarify anything that needs it."

So she described driving to the construction site, finding Ruffino waiting, and everything she could remember about their exchange. When she got to the moment where he had been shot, she faltered. "I never saw the bodyguard draw his weapon," she said. "I was talking to Ruffino and one minute he was there and the next minute…" She shook her head, the horror of the moment once more replaying in her mind.

"What happened then?" Sanderlin prompted.

She drank more water, not wanting to remember, but forcing herself to do so. "I asked why he shot Ruffino, then he aimed the gun at me. I was frozen in place, but I guess some part of me—the part that wanted to survive—took over. I dived over that wall and scrambled into the culvert. I don't know why. It would have been easy for one of the two men to follow me, but I just wanted to get away from the bullets. And then I guess the SWAT team showed up, and everything was okay." She closed her eyes. "Thank God it was okay."

Sanderlin glanced down at a notebook she hadn't even noticed until now. "A little before he was shot, Ruffino said something about radiation levels. What did he mean by that?"

She shook her head. "I don't know. Did he mean radiation at the mine? Isn't that what my father was trying to get people to pay attention to?"

"The initial reports TDC submitted to the EPA—the ones your father supposedly authored—showed very low levels of radioactivity at the Mary Lee mine," Hud said. "The same levels you'd find in most rocky areas around here, and not enough to pose any danger. But later measurements your father took, after the mitigation work began, showed much higher levels of radioactivity."

"And the EPA fined TDC for falsifying their initial reports," Audra said. "And TDC blamed my father. But then later, the EPA declared the mine site okay. I remember TDC had a big press conference to announce that all the toxic stuff had been cleared."

Hud sat back. "I've been going over all this in my head," he said. "When Ruffino was talking about safe levels and everything being taken care of, I wonder if he wasn't referring to the mine, but to the school?"

"You mean there was radioactive material at the school?" Sanderlin asked.

Hud nodded. "TDC donated the land for that

school. What if they did it not because they were especially civic-minded, but because they discovered it was hot and they needed to get rid of it? They dug up as much of the radioactive rock as they could and hauled it up to the Mary Lee mine, where they planned to gradually get rid of it as part of the mitigation process."

"But my father figured out what they were doing," Audra said.

"Right," Hud said. "And he either confronted Ruffino with his findings, or Ruffino or someone else at TDC found out that he knew the truth, and they threatened him—or they threatened you—and Dane decided he'd be better off going into hiding and fighting TDC covertly."

"Then what did they do with the radioactive rock after they removed it from the mine?" Audra asked.

"They dumped it on public land," Hud said. "In the Curecanti Recreation Area. We thought it was construction debris all along, and it was, but most of it, maybe all of it, was stuff they had dumped at the mine, then hauled to wilderness land."

"Ruffino said they had bribed people. Inspectors, maybe. Regulators." She rubbed her temples. Her head throbbed, making it difficult to think.

"It sounds like TDC has spent a fortune in bribes," Sanderlin said.

"How can they afford to keep it up?" Hud asked. "It's not like they made that much profit from building the elementary school. They didn't get anything but a tax write-off for the land they donated. The fines the EPA levied ate into their income from the mine cleanup."

"I think something else must be going on," Audra said.

The two men stared at her. "Ruffino talked about an operation," she said. "He said if I talked I could ruin 'the whole operation.' And when I suggested working with him, using my day care center as a cover, he said he'd have to talk to the people above him. Does he mean Terrell, Davis and Compton?"

"You may be onto something," Sanderlin said. "It could be the two men who accompanied Ruffino to the meetup with you weren't so much there as bodyguards, but to keep him from saying the wrong thing. He may have been killed to silence him."

The queasy feeling washed over her again. Hud's hand on her shoulder steadied her.

"Thank you for your help." Sanderlin slid back his chair and stood. "We may have more questions later, but Officer Hudson can take you home now."

Neither she nor Hud spoke on the drive home. She sat in the passenger seat of her car, welcoming the numbness, afraid of the storm of emotions that might wash over her if she allowed herself to feel. Hud pulled into her driveway, and she got out of the car and followed him up the walk.

Once inside, she was about to head to the bathroom when he took her hand and pulled her close. "I love you," he said. "I should have said it before, but I can't wait any longer. I love you, and I was so afraid for you this afternoon—and so proud, too."

The words surrounded her and melted into her and soothed her like a healing balm. She looked into his eyes and saw how much he meant to her with those three little syllables, and in spite of everything, she couldn't help smiling. "I love you, too," she said. "I can hardly believe it happened, in the midst of all of this chaos, but I do."

"Believe it," he said, and kissed her—a long, deep kiss that made her feel as if she were floating above all the horribleness of the last few hours.

AUDRA INSISTED ON going in to work Friday morning, over Hud's objections. "I'll do much better if I focus on the children and my job, instead of sitting here brooding." She kissed his cheek and gathered her purse and messenger bag. "And I really think the worst is over. You'll see."

Hud didn't share her optimism, and said as much when he reported to Ranger Brigade headquarters. "If Ruffino was only acting at the behest of others, Audra won't be safe," he told the commander when everyone had gathered for the morning briefing. "We need to go after Terrell, Davis and Compton. I have a hard time believing Ruffino orchestrated all of this without them knowing about it."

"Terrell, Davis and Compton have issued a statement saying they had no knowledge of any of this and are appalled, horrified, etcetera," Sanderlin said.

"You don't believe that, do you?" Hud asked.

"We don't have any evidence showing their involvement," Sanderlin said. "The man who survived the shooting, Alex Ballantine, says Ruffino hired them as bodyguards because he said he had a meeting with a 'dangerous, shady character' and needed protection. Ballantine said Ruffino told them he was being blackmailed by this person and was afraid."

"So why did Ballantine's partner kill Ruffino?" Dance asked.

"Ballantine says the other man—Derek Capshaw—was just a guy he knows from the gym they both belong to. He says Ruffino pulled a knife on Audra and Capshaw must have decided on his own to protect the woman, who they both figured out pretty quick wasn't a threat."

"Audra didn't say anything about a knife," Hud said.

"Ballantine says she may not have seen it. And she's probably in shock."

"So where is the knife now?" Beck asked.

"If must have been lost in the scuffle," Sanderlin said.

"I think he's lying," Hud said.

"He's sticking to his story," Sanderlin said. "And he's coming up clean—no record for him or Capshaw."

Hud started to object again, but Sanderlin continued. "The bottom line is, this isn't our case anymore," Sanderlin said. "The shooting happened on county property, and it's their jurisdiction. They're probably going to press charges against Ballantine, but as far as they're concerned—and as far as the evidence shows—this was all Mitch Ruffino's doing. He was in charge of both the mine cleanup and the school construction, and TDC's statement emphasizes that he had complete autonomy. TDC is an international company, and the partners do not oversee day-to-day operations of their various offices."

Hud exchanged looks with others around the table. Some of them clearly shared his frustration. "Our job is to locate Dane Trask," Sanderlin continued. "That hasn't changed."

"When we find Trask, what then?" Dance asked.

"Maybe he'll having something to tell us," Sanderlin said. "Maybe he won't. But we have to do our job."

As far as Hud was concerned, he had a new job now—protecting the woman he loved.

He met Audra at the school at the end of the day. "How did it go?" he asked. "Any hassles from the press?"

"None. The news stories only mention that Mitch Ruffino was killed in 'an altercation at the school.' No mention of me at all." She smiled. "I'm hoping it stays that way. I'm guessing TDC will do everything they can to hush up this whole episode."

"You look pretty cheerful," he said. He had expected her to still be distraught and worried.

"Take a look at this." She motioned him over to her desk and pulled up a website on her computer.

He leaned in to get a better look. Montrose ISD Cancels New Elementary School Project read the headline. He skimmed the article that followed. The school district was halting construction due to "cost overruns and population projections that the school is not necessary at this time." According to the article, TDC had agreed to refund the money the district had paid so far and dismantle construction. The district thanked TDC for its cooperation and civic-mindedness, and cited the move as an example of the district's commitment to fiscal responsibility.

Hud looked at Audra. "That didn't take long," he said.

"I think TDC is very anxious to rebuild their reputation and make this all go away," she said. "Oh, and I received these this morning." She led him into the outer office, where a large flower arrangement took up much of a side table.

"Who sent those?" Hud asked.

"TDC! Along with a note apologizing for Mitch Ruffino's behavior and reassurances that they had nothing to do with any of this. They offered to assist me in any way they could."

"Assist you with what?"

"They didn't say. I think they're anxious to ensure I don't sue them. Oh, and of course, they're not suing me anymore, either. That was apparently Ruffino's doing, as well."

"Do you believe them?" he asked.

"I think I do." She touched the petals of a large red rose. "We've said all along none of this really made financial sense. And Ruffino has always been the one speaking out against my father, not Terrell, Davis or Compton."

He slipped an arm around her. Maybe she was right, and he'd been letting his emotions, and his suspicious nature, get in the way of common sense. "If the new elementary school won't be opened, then the new day care center won't, either."

"I should feel bad for Jana, but I don't really," Audra said. "I hired a new teacher today for her class—one of the moms who has been subbing wants the job. And our new anti-bullying curriculum starts next week."

She smiled up at him. The woman who had faced down death yesterday, who had seen her reputation shredded in the last week, had bounced back to this happy, optimistic person making plans for the future. "You're incredible, do you know that?" he asked.

"My dad taught me to focus on the things I could control and to look to the future," she said. "I resented his advice a lot when I was younger, but I guess I took it to heart after all."

"We're still looking for your father," he said.

"He's bound to hear about Ruffino's death soon," she said. "If he hasn't already. He'll be back, I'm sure of it." She hugged him close. "There's something else I'm sure of, too."

"Oh, what is that?"

"I'm sure that you're the man I'm meant to be with."

"Is that more planning for the future?"

Her eyes met his, full of warmth and an optimism he found infectious. "I'm ready to put all this behind us," she said. "If you're willing."

"I'm willing," he said.

* * * * *

Don't miss the gripping conclusion to
The Ranger Brigade: Rocky Mountain Manhunt
by Cindi Myers
when Presumed Deadly *goes on sale next month!*

And look for the previous books in the series:

Investigation in Black Canyon
Mountain of Evidence

Available now wherever Harlequin Intrigue
books are sold!

WE HOPE YOU ENJOYED
THIS BOOK FROM

H HARLEQUIN

INTRIGUE

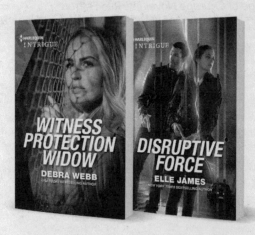

Seek thrills. Solve crimes. Justice served.

Dive into action-packed stories that will keep you
on the edge of your seat. Solve the crime
and deliver justice at all costs.

6 NEW BOOKS AVAILABLE EVERY MONTH!

SPECIAL EXCERPT FROM

ⓗ HARLEQUIN

INTRIGUE

*LAPD detective Jake McAllister has his work cut out
for him trying to identify and capture a serial killer
hunting women. The last thing he needs is victims' rights
advocate Kyra Chase included on his task force. He
senses trouble whenever she's around, and not just to
his hardened heart. It also seems she might have a very
personal connection to this most challenging of cases…*

*Keep reading for a sneak peek at
The Setup,
the first book in A Kyra and Jake Investigation,
from Carol Ericson.*

He'd recognize that voice anywhere, even though he'd
heard it live and in person just a few times and never
so…forceful. He believed her, but he had no intention
of letting her off the hook so easily.

He raised his hands. "I'm LAPD Detective
Jake McAllister. Are you all right?"

A sudden gust of wind carried her sigh down the trail
toward him.

"It…it's Kyra Chase. I'm sorry. I'm putting away my
weapon."

Lowering his hands, he said, "Is it okay for me to
move now?"

"Of course. I didn't realize... I thought you were..."

"The killer coming back to his dump site?" He flicked on the flashlight in his hand and continued down the trail, his shoes scuffing over dirt and pebbles. "He wouldn't do that—at least not so soon after the kill."

When he got within two feet of her, he skimmed the beam over her body, her dark clothing swallowing up the light until it reached her blond hair. "I didn't mean to scare you, but what are you doing here?"

"Probably the same thing you are." She hung on to the strap of her purse, her hand inches from the gun pocket.

"I'm the lead detective on the case, and I'm doing some follow-up investigation."

"Believe it or not, Detective, I have my own prep work that I like to do before meeting a victim's family. I want to have as much information as possible when talking to them. I'm sure you can understand that."

"Sure, I can. And call me Jake."